THE STORY OF ISOBEL KUHN

THE STORY OF
ISOBEL KUHN

One Vision Only

CAROLYN CANFIELD

HODDER AND STOUGHTON
and
THE OVERSEAS MISSIONARY FELLOWSHIP

British Library Cataloguing in Publication Data

Canfield, Carolyn
One vision only
    1. Kuhn, Isobel   2. Missionaries – China – Biography
    I. Title   II. Story of Isobel Kuhn
266'.023'0924   BV3427.K8

ISBN 0 340 24607 3

Reproduced, printed and bound in Great Britain for Hodder and Stoughton Limited, Mill Road, Dunton Green, Sevenoaks, Kent by Cox & Wyman Ltd., London, Reading and Fakenham

CONTENTS

Part Three

THE VISION REALIZED

HIGH IN HER MOUNTAINS

"SEE that trail starting up the slope?"

John Kuhn's broad hand waved our attention to a point across the valley.

We nodded: "That one winding into the foot hills?"

"That's right!" he assented. "Keep climbing up that trail for six days, and you'll find Isobel."

"Six *days* through that wilderness?"

"Yes, and Danny is with her in the Lisuland shanty."

As we stood there at Wa Yao, my husband and I were far down the Burma Road in southwest China. The vividly green valley before us was scalloped with wooded hills and faced with blue mountains of great height.

So we were on Isobel Kuhn's doorstep! Her writing, like strong cords, had helped weave the primitive tribes into the affections of Christians on several continents. Thousands of people, we among them, enjoyed her letters and books; laughing, crying, and praying over them. Her love for the Lisu was infectious.

And this was our nearest point of approach to Isobel Kuhn!

Her husband's longing to hit the home trail spoke through his eyes. We understood. We too felt our hearts pushing us towards Isobel. But six days' struggle up those heights? We could not make it! Already our little party lagged behind schedule. Stretching before us was the further overland journey. It was to cover several thousands of miles, partly over Communist infested roads.

So, instead of striking out on foot to Isobel, we just had to go jeeping on without even a How-do-you-do.

It was quite impossible even to let Isobel know that our hands were waving in her direction. She had no telephone, no telegraph, even her post office was distant by a day's journey.

With John, our party pressed on towards Paoshan city, and

the China-Burma border where a Lisu Bible Conference was planned. Soon more than a hundred tribespeople would come filing through the wilds from their scattered villages with a great appetite for the Living Bread. John Kuhn's messages were a spiritual treat to any audience, anywhere. From his lips God's Word poured out as readily in Chinese and Lisu as in English. No wonder the tribal Christians received him with singing and wept when he left!

John's work as China Inland Mission superintendent for West Yunnan kept him away from home for indefinitely long stretches. During her husband's absence, Isobel was in her mountains, tied to the small boy as well as to the work at the mission station.

At that time, 1949, the John Kuhns with their fellow-worker, Charles Peterson, were based at Village of Olives. Their shanty, as they called it, was large and clean. But it was not much more embellished than the bamboo huts of the thousands of their parish, or of the four hundred pathetically poor tribespeople immediately around them. Their furniture evolved out of packing cases. The water supply dribbled in through bamboo tubes. In that rugged area there was not a wheeled vehicle of any kind, nor a stretch of road where one could be used. In many places the trails were so narrow that even mules could not travel with a pack. Almost no supplies were procurable and shops or markets were non-existent. Mail was carried only by their own special messenger. Their mountain neighbourhood was full of Lisu who were strangers to God but well acquainted with such things as opium, hard liquor and filthy lust.

When, during furlough, the hardship of such living conditions was commented upon by a special friend, Isobel responded, "Oh, it's a bit hard, but it's nothing compared with the spiritual luxury of the place."

Observing her manner of life, the godless nicknamed Isobel, "God's Daughter." But the Christian Lisu called her "Ma-ma," the Lady Teacher. She was all that these appellations implied: a lady by culture and a teacher by profession. She was also an obedient child of God, keenly alert to that too frequently over-looked part of His final commission: "Go . . . preach the gospel to every creature." . . . "*Teaching them to observe all things whatsoever I have commanded you.*"

It was Isobel's delight to gather groups of young Christians for special Bible study during the weeks when rain gave them leisure from crop tilling. She added practical instruction in righteous living, homecraft, and child care to reading classes and well prepared Bible lessons.

When sessions of the Rainy Season Bible School closed, the students returned to their far distant villages, happily chatting over their experiences. So Ma-ma's ministry was multiplied through the mountains.

Isobel was in the midst of one of her Rainy Season Bible Schools while our party was hurrying westward. From her mountain perch she regarded the Burma Road as civilization, and it was, by contrast with her isolation! To us first-timers, however, it seemed really remote. Its exotic wild flowers, crags and canyons thrilled us. So did its multiple hazards! Winding, grinding and skidding, the jeep faltered over the dirt surface. Our self-imposed speed limit was 20 miles per hour, necessary both for comfort and safety. But 20 miles per day was the rate at which Isobel and her husband first passed that same way, long before there ever had been a thought of the Burma Road.

Sometimes ominous loneliness clung to the atmosphere. We were approaching a national boundary where smugglers and bandits thrive, and these were no hobgoblins of imagination! Besides, at that time, there were bands of vagrant soldiers who, with only their guns left in their hands in lieu of pay, had been discharged from regular service. To make an easy living, they preyed upon their hard working fellow countrymen.

Most to be feared of all desperadoes, however, were the Reds. Like cayenne pepper, they had mixed themselves into the political pot of this loosely governed area. The resulting stew was such that the peaceable Chinese populace could not even distinguish its flavour. Were their towns seething with bandits, Reds or wandering soldiers? At times they did not know. They only knew the mess was hot and evil smelling!

A great time to be bumping along the Burma Road! Yet if we felt too near the hot-pot, what about Isobel? Most of the time she lived on the edge of danger twenty-four hours a day.

Far away in America, Kathryn Kuhn, then a student at Wheaton College, Illinois, wondered why no letters came from her parents. With tears, she heard that the city of Paoshan had been taken while her father was there. Rumours started that her parents had been captured.

Rumours and more rumours!

Rumours filled the Salween and Mekong canyons in southwest China also. Like steam from a boiling cauldron, the fumes of war rose from the valleys far below the lone woman in the mountains. Soon Isobel also heard that Paoshan had fallen. Weeks added more and more suspense. No word from her husband!

"Where is John?" she wrote. "We don't know. He apparently can't get word to us, and we can't get word to anybody . . . we have no stamps and can only hazard a hope that the missionaries at —— (in Upper Burma) will mail these letters out for us." "Cut off," Isobel headed that letter, explaining that contacts with the world outside the mountains had been completely severed by all the evil men of the neighbourhood, working under Red command.

Meanwhile John returned with us from the inspiring Bible conference at the Burma border. But while we jeeped back along the dangerously deserted road to the comparative safety of civilization, John got stuck in Paoshan. He was refused a pass. Warring factions blocked his way home to his wife in the distant village. Then followed promiscuous shooting, anarchy and bloodshed. Three complete changes of government took place in quick succession. It was John's "two months in a robbers' nest," as he called that ordeal.

Nearer and nearer the turmoil boiled up into the mountains towards Isobel. She wrote, "They (the Reds) crossed the river to our side of the Salween, just one short day's journey away. Next they announced their intention of coming to our Village of Olives. Everyone surmises that they are coming to get the white missionaries." Of "white missionaries" there were then only two —Isobel Kuhn and Charles Peterson, several days' travel from their nearest white neighbours.

Circumstances had a grim face, even though Christian Lisu were quite ready to defend their missionaries with their lives.

"But our hearts are at peace," Isobel wrote, "for Philippians 4:6-7 has always been our trust." ("Be careful—anxious—for nothing; but in everything by prayer and supplication with thanksgiving, let your requests be made known unto God. And the peace of God, which passeth all understanding, shall keep your hearts and minds through Christ Jesus.")

The tone of the whole letter verifies her claim of having a peaceful heart. Her anxious readers were even conscious of the twinkle in her eye as she wrote: "Needless to say, life is interesting . . . especially to one small boy who dreams of the Sugar Creek Gang every night and longs for a gun to go shoot bears."

As she rode high in her perilous mountains, she kept teaching and mothering and writing. But, by nature, Isobel Miller Kuhn was full of fears—and frail bodied, besides. How did such a person manage bravely to face such a life full of mountains?

After studying her character rather minutely, it seems to me that Isobel Kuhn kept before her one vision only. Her basic life secret is well summed up in the scripture which says "Who *through faith* . . . wrought righteousness, obtained promises . . . out of weakness (she was) made strong."

Part One

THE VISION SIGHTED

CHAPTER ONE

DADDY'S GIRL

THE Millers' first child, Murray, was two and a half years old when Isobel came into the world. One day the little fellow impulsively tried to pick up his newborn sister. Finding her quite too heavy an armful to carry downstairs to his mother, he left her, hanging head down, on the edge of the bed.

No one in the house knew of her plight. But God, having a special purpose for that life, just then prompted the nurse to run upstairs. There she discovered the week-old baby girl, blue-faced and scarcely breathing! Immediate attention soon restored the tiny heart to its normal rhythm.

Who could have guessed that the saving of little Isobel's life would have such significance to thousands of forgotten people of the world? Not even Samuel Miller himself, though known far and wide as a visionary, then dreamed of his infant daughter's potentialities—how far this baby's feet would travel, and how wide an influence her small round fist would wield when she later grasped a pen!

She was born in her maternal grandmother's home at 60 Henry Street, Toronto, Canada. Octavia Selina Irish actually was from Ireland and a woman of great character. Of course, it was for her that Isobel was named Selina.

That was December 17, 1901.

Such a genial young fellow as Sam P. Miller must have had many a friend to congratulate him that day on the birth of his second child. And no doubt he was heartily thanking God for the safe arrival of this baby; praying too, that he might be a good father to her. Though fallible as any of us, he was nevertheless, quite personally acquainted with his Father in heaven, and through the years repeatedly showed himself a true father, with a feeling of responsibility to God for her life. So Isobel Selina Miller came into the world with a real heritage, the greatest parents can give a child; that of godliness.

Perhaps, as he gazed at his infant daughter, "S.P." wondered if she would take after his side of the family. Would she be short like himself and his plump little Irish mother, Nanette Transdell Miller? Or would she stretch out, long and lean like his tall father?

When Samuel himself was born, his parents were home missionaries among the sailors of Liverpool. His father, a Presbyterian clergyman, founded a home for seamen's widows and their children. But when Sam was about twelve years old, his parents went to Canada. On a small Ontario farm the boy grew up, while his father farmed and preached.

In the pioneer missionary family, of course, there was no money for higher education. In spite of this, Sam's older brother, Dr. Joseph Ormsley Miller, worked his way through the University of Toronto. Later he founded Ridley College for boys in St. Catherine's, Ontario, becoming its first principal. He helped Sam enter Wycliffe College, for Sam had the intention of qualifying himself for the ministry in the Church of England. Perhaps the young fellow was too full of fun to be industrious. At any rate, he left college after only a year's work. Later he applied to the British and Foreign Bible Society to go to China as a colporteur. He was accepted, but something happened to cancel that particular ship's sailing and Sam never reached the foreign field.

While living in Toronto "S.P." and his chum, Fred Irish, attended the Presbyterian Church of which Dr. McTavish was then pastor. One Sunday evening at Christian Endeavour, Sam met Fred's pretty sister, Alice Irish. Alice's blue eyes and artistic temperament promptly did something to Sam's heart!

Alice, born in Valleyfield, Quebec, was half Irish, but the Irish half did not come through her father, who bore that as his surname. Her mother's family, boasted descent from a disinherited son of the Earl of Enniskillen. The tradition was never verified, however, and when Alice's sister was once asked to corroborate Alice's version of the earl story, she laughingly retorted; "Oh! Alice was always romantic!"

Whether or not she was romantic, Alice was certainly very musical. Studying at the Toronto Conservatory of Music, she became the medallist in only her second year. When she was just about to be graduated, tragedy struck her life. Her father's investments failed. As a private banker, he conscientiously protected his clients to the full extent of his personal fortune. Then he went into bankruptcy. He soon died heartbroken. That same year Alice's brother Fred died of tuberculosis. Then Alice herself suffered a breakdown.

With such burdens weighing Alice's young life, it is easy to see how she gladly accepted the love of her brother's close friend, kindly Samuel Persse Miller; Persse, she always called him. Alice was 23 when they were married.

Their baby Isobel came into the world with much natural enduement from both sides of the family: the personal magnetism of her father, the artistic sensitivity of her mother, intellectual capacity, business ability, Irish wit from both sides of the house. But she was Alice's baby in temperament.

The little girl with a sprinkle of freckles on her tilted nose grew into an attractive child. She soon shaped into the pattern of her paternal aunt—brown starry eyes, smooth dark hair, and slim lines. A certain set to her mouth prophesied the determination that drove her through life. But her pretty smile was always ready, especially when she saw her father approaching. She was Daddy's Girl from the first. Murray was his mother's choice. Family friction was the inevitable result. Though Sam and Alice Miller loved the Lord, and made a genuine effort to give their children a Christian upbringing, they showed some of the human inconsistencies common to all of us.

Isobel and her brother were near enough of an age to be companionable. Murray remembered their childhood as being different from most youngsters. "Dad was working for the Victor Electric Company. He helped build their first X-ray machine. His speciality was electric therapeutics, and that meant setting up agencies all over the United States and Canada. Isobel and I, with our parents, were always moving to different cities—Pittsburgh, Cleveland, Philadelphia, St. Louis—going to new schools and Sunday schools, and making new friends. It was rough on our education for countries and states have such different standards. This mobility did teach us, however, how to mix and make friends without too much difficulty—I can remember, when we lived in St. Louis, Dad would often come home late. Isobel and I would be asleep when he would come into our room and shout, 'Ice-cream!' Isobel would open her mouth while her eyes were still shut! As long as money was rolling in, we had the best of everything."

Of course the little girl fondly regarded her indulgent father as the most wonderful man in the world. "He was extravagantly generous, and so as a child I adored my daddy who never came home from a trip without bringing us lovely gifts. Mother would often rather have had the money than the expensive pocketbook, jewelled comb or gold locket but of course I was too young to understand that. My father never had any conscience about going into debt especially if he owned any assets, a house or furniture. But as I grew up I had a horror of debt. I think this feeling must have come to me through my mother."

S.P. with his great sense of humour and hearty laugh made a good salesman. His sales talk and personal magnetism were convincing, and he verily expected that his pot of gold would appear with the next rainbow. "Son," he would say to Murray, "you may never be a millionaire but try to live like one." His son's own comment was, "Most of the time Dad made real good money, but could he ever spend it!"

When money flowed in freely but rolled out like a river at flood, the young mother anxiously tried to build dykes around pools of it for the family's everyday needs.

In these circumstances, Mrs. Miller taught the children to pray for their daily food. As Murray tells it: "During 1910 we lived in Pittsburgh. Dad was on the road and we never knew where our next meal was coming from. I can remember our kneeling and asking God to send us some money as there wasn't any food in the house. Always the next day a letter would come with enough money to tide us over."

These were valuable lessons for each of the four Millers. How better could God show them that He was the real source of their supply, a Heavenly Father whose eye is towards the righteous, and His ear is open to their cry! What more practical way for the children to learn to run to Him with all their troubles?

And so Dad's daughter was beginning her ABCs in the primary schools where the Holy Spirit is the teacher. Did her primer's first page look something like this?

Lesson I

A. Ask God. *He can do anything.*
B. Believe God. *He can be trusted.*
C. Come to God. *He loves you.*

Later, as God's daughter, Isobel was thankful that her Instructor started her early in His school, for the lessons were not so simple as they had at first seemed to be. These ABCs needed much reviewing. Yet, even to a child, God stooped to demonstrate His loving care, showing her that though her clever daddy might unintentionally fail her, her Heavenly Father would not.

Doubtless it was the very warmth of Dad's heart that melted the money out of his pocket, for Isobel said: "As a child, I was quite accustomed to people I hardly knew hailing me to tell me how kind my father had been to them. Once a perfect stranger stopped me in the middle of a busy downtown street to tell me such a story, with tears."

For a few years the Millers lived with Grandma Irish or near her in their own home. On visits, too, her arms were always open to them. The youngsters loved her dearly. But a parting had to come. When Isobel was about eleven, her parents made the big decision to venture across the continent and settle in Vancouver, B.C. The spectacle of the Canadian Rockies was Isobel's first introduction to the wonders of giant mountains!

For the next twelve years she could always look up at the great "Lions" proudly presiding on their peaks above Vancouver harbour. Now that the roving family had finally taken root, the Millers lived in their own substantial house at 342 Seventeenth Avenue. At school Isobel applied herself to her studies, and she soon emerged at the head of her class. Her mother gave her piano lessons, read and told her delightful stories. "Mother was one of the best storytellers I have ever heard," said Isobel. She pleasantly pictured a long remembered phase of their home life: "As Mother, at her piano, improvised in the evening firelight while the rest of us listened eagerly, Daddy would say, 'Now Alice, that's lovely. You must write that down tomorrow morning; it will go well with the boys at the mission.' (We used to go as a family to one of the Rescue Mission halls in the slums—Daddy to preach, Mother to play, Brother Murray and I to sing to those poor human derelicts.) Those were the days when God added all other things, too, because His kingdom was first sought. . . . In his prime, Father was a soul winner."

For their family the Millers built a commodious resort home at White Rock, beside the blue Pacific. There they had the best of entertainment. It was the homemade kind, sparkling waters to play in by day and the fun of singing around a big bonfire on the beach at night. On Sunday evenings on the pier under the setting sun, they would hold gospel meetings. There the swish of the ocean made the hymns sound far better than in any church.

What pure fun to store up in the memory banks of the young brother and sister! Murray drew on these deposits when he was bogged down in the trench mud of France during the first world war. And such memories steadied Isobel, too, as her battles began in the spiritual realm.

Even as a girl, Isobel met frustrations with strong reactions. There were rebellious times when she wanted to run away from home. Usually, however, she appeared to be just a bright, happy child, and everyone supposed she was a Christian. "Of course!" they thought, "isn't her father an elder in the Presbyterian Church . . . a lay preacher? Isn't her mother a leading light in the missionary society? And Isobel is such a *good* girl!"

Church and Sunday school, church and Sunday school; Isobel was always there. Daily she took a few minutes to read the Bible and say her prayers. Yet no one seemed to realize that she was simply being carried along by the momentum of her parent's example. "Born of the flesh," but not yet "born of the Spirit"! Her experience did not include obedience to the authoritative Word of Jesus Christ: "Ye must be born again."

But did such a girl as Isobel Miller need to be "born again"?

She was soon to enter into the conflict that eventually answered that vital question for her.

CHAPTER TWO

ALL IN A WHIRL

CLEVER and talented, the girl flew ahead of others with her characteristic ability to excel.

On entering high school, Isobel won the Governor-General's medal for all British Columbia. Later at the University of British Columbia, she consistently won the highest marks. Besides, her brother comments: "She was an excellent actress and later toured widely with the University Players' Club. She could easily have become professional, only Mother didn't approve. As for dancing, there are few girls I have ever found equal to Isobel." Though "Mother didn't approve," it was Mother who had previously seen to it that her daughter studied elocution and dancing. Mrs. Miller had always trained her children to love the Lord. Yet, as they grew older, she wanted them to "move in good society." This was the aspiration that unwittingly pushed Isobel into a crowd where Christ was ignored.

Isobel did not realize that hidden in the gay whirl of the campus was a battleground. She did not suspect that the popularity and pleasure she craved could lead her into treacherous booby traps. There were so many attractive things scattered within each reach! They all seemed to be labelled, "Fun, and all the good things of this world." She did not realize that by these, her soul's enemy planned to trip her into a pit of worldliness, and snap the trap on her for life.

Isobel tells it all with such fascinating frankness in *By Searching*[1], that only selected bits of those important years need to be reviewed in this story.

The battle began in one of Isobel's freshman classes. It was started by a professor's affable scorn for what he considered a myth: the Genesis story of life's origin. Assuming once for all that no *thinker* could believe the Bible, he questioned: "Is there

[1] China Inland Mission, 1957.

anyone here who believes there is a heaven or hell?" Isobel, in a roomful of students, found that only her own and one other hand were raised. The two extended arms looked as lonesome as two solitary telephone posts in a wide desert! Then came his teasing sneer that slid Isobel down into the wide expanse of drifting sand: "Oh, you just believe that because your papa and your mama told you so!"

That did it!

It was like decisive Isobel that she made up her mind quickly. At the end of her walk home from class, she had come to the conclusion that she would not accept a theory of life which she had not proved personally.

If only she had turned to the old proverb from the Book she was so lightly discarding! Right there in black and white was a warning and solution for her immediate need: "The fear of man bringeth a snare, but whoso putteth his trust in the Lord shall be safe." By trusting Him, what emotional misery she could have saved herself! But no! She must figure things out for herself.

And so she walked into the deceiver's trap, and the snare snapped.

"Ignorant of the end to which that attitude would lead me . . . I was only conscious of a sudden welcome freedom from old duties."

For a while, life drifted along pleasantly.

Since it was a popular thing to question "the ancient faith," Isobel in her doubts, had plenty of company. As one of the crowd, she was regarded as a modern and intelligent person.

Her Christian foundation, however, held her to belief in Jesus Christ as a historical character. "Even though I had ceased to seek Him, His purity and holiness made me hate besmirching things. The effects of my home training still stayed with me. So when I broke with the old religious habits and frankly went into the world, I still was choosey in what I did. I never smoked, and I did not drink—all because my father and my mother had taught me so. In the gay group at college, I was considered a good girl, and even a Christian! I knew myself that I wasn't. Urgently my mother pleaded with me to attend the Y.W.C.A. I went, but was bored, so dropped it."

Dancing and the Players' Club (the amateur dramatic club of

the university) absorbed most of Isobel's spare time. Gifted in acting comedy parts, she soon won life membership in the club, an unusual honour for a freshman.

More honours came. The popular girl was elected secretary of the Students' Council in her second year, at that time the highest elective position possible for a co-ed. This threw her in with the leading students, and before long she met Ben.

Vivacity and wit like a playing arc light drew many admirers to the girl with the teasing Irish eyes. But when Ben's long legs strode across Isobel's path he no doubt looked every inch a hero. He was several years older than she, and a returned soldier from World War I. Besides, he starred on the Varsity rugby and basket-ball teams.

"We went together for nearly two years," she relates, "and my path was perceptibly downgrade."

Then, one day in Isobel's senior year, her chum came to her with a story that upset her completely. "Isobel," she said, "I think I should tell you something, even though it may hurt. Everybody but you knows your fiancé is not loyal to you. He is taking another girl out behind your back." Isobel found herself writhing under the unwelcome facts as if they were heavy heels grinding her into the dust.

She saw it now! With the outflowing of her first love, she had laid her very heart at Ben's feet, and he had walked on it.

When she confronted him, Ben responded: "Isobel, you don't suppose, do you, that after we're married, I'm not going to take other women out sometimes?"

She was stunned.

"Then we part!" she whispered.

Isobel found herself wounded in the enemy's trap, the whirling rubble of all her air castles falling about her. Was this the promised "fun and all the good things of this life"?

"Pride wounded me, love afflicted me, sleep departed from me. I was working hard, I had signed up for the honours course in English Literature which entailed more work than a mere pass degree. I needed to sleep at night, but couldn't.

"One night when all the house had been asleep for hours, I was still tossing. Dad, for days, had been sympathetically silent about my troubles. But that night sensing my need, he came into my bedroom. There he knelt down beside me, and prayed God to help me."

" 'Thanks, Dad,' I said wearily, 'I know you mean it well, but it doesn't go beyond the ceiling, you know.' I never forgot the groan with which he turned and left the room."

Her father had a long wait for the answer to that prayer of his. But, despite Isobel's unbelief, his groaning surely went higher than the ceiling that night. A real father, he longed to lift his daughter in his sturdy arms and transfer her into the Everlasting Arms of the God of all comfort! But the dust of despair had so blinded her that she struck out against all proffered help.

Then breaking into another dark night, the most climactic fight of Isobel Miller's life came rushing upon her.

Overwork, sleeplessness, a heavy heart. These added up to desperation.

Oh! to be done with this unhappy life!

Slyly, the Tempter pulled her out of bed and pointed towards a little bottle in the bathroom. The vial was marked with skull and crossbones. But with her hand on the door, the Lord stopped her. In the next room her father moaned in his sleep. Startled by the sound, Isobel suddenly realized what her tragic death might mean to this dear father.

"Daddy!" she swallowed a sob. "How could I do anything to break your heart!" The thought turned her back to the edge of her bed. There she sank in despair, experiencing what she later called the darkest moment of her life. "I didn't want to live and I couldn't die."

Finally, with hands uplifted, she whispered into the black shadows, "God (if there be a God), if You will prove to me that You are, and give me peace, I will give You my whole life—do anything You ask, go anywhere You send me." Then she climbed into bed and pulled the blankets over her.

Immediately she fell asleep and slept like a baby. Next morning, true to her bargain, but still hardly believing that God had met her, she decided to search for God through the teachings of Christ in the New Testament. Her Bible was on a shelf. There it lay unused, just as it was when her father gave it to her on the day of her high school graduation. She began praying again, too. But not before three months of this had passed could she point to unmistakable evidences that God was answering. He even helped her when she prayed for trivial and unworthy things— dates for dances, bids for parties!

She still never went to church nor spoke of her spiritual experience. Yet her parents sensed a change in her.

One Sunday afternoon, because of her mother's urging, Isobel went with her to a Bible study class at the Vancouver Bible School. She found the teacher, Professor Ellis, a remarkable combination of conservative scholarship and Christian kindliness. "Watching the radiance of his face," she said, "I instinctively knew he had personal dealings with God, and I decided that this was the preacher for me. . . . I was willing to learn from such a man as Professor Ellis."

After one of the first of those Bible classes, a white-haired gentlemen, her father's friend, said to her, "Isobel, I'm glad to see you here." Then with eyes flooded with tears he added, "I've been praying for you for seven years." The girl's eyes overflowed also, as she tried to thank him. She explained the tears by saying: "It was about seven years since I had decided to dance and go in for worldly things against my father's pleadings."

A pleading father, a concerned mother, a sincere Bible teacher, a praying elderly friend! Perhaps it was the memory of such spiritual helpers as these that in later years made Isobel so keen to help tempted young people with their problems.

Only a few months before, in her middle-of-the-night anguish, she had cried out to Someone whom she hardly believed existed. If He would only prove Himself to her! Amazingly enough, it was as if the Lord stood listening at her door, key in hand. He was only waiting to hear her sincere cry so that He might release her from the dungeon of her doubts and despair. While she imagined herself searching for God, it was really God who had been seeking her!

"True worshippers shall worship the Father in spirit and in truth: For the Father seeketh such to worship Him. God is a spirit."

This she had learned out of a long, dark night of personal experience. But she did not arrive at spiritual maturity all in a day.

CHAPTER THREE

A NEW LOOK

WHEN she received her B.A. degree she was twenty-one and one of the most popular girls in the university; tall and slim, with a quantity of dark hair, and beautifully arched eyebrows. There was a new look dawning in her brown eyes.

Now it was not because her father and her mother told her so, that she believed in God! Her four years at college completed, she came out with conclusions quite at variance with her atheistic professor.

That was in May, 1922.

Her university credits, plus a few months of Normal School, put a teacher's certificate in her hand. It had been her ambition to be a dean of women and teach English in a university. But her youth and inexperience stood between her and even a city high school job. Although she might have taught in a country high school, her mother did not want her to go out of the city to live; so she settled for a position in Vancouver, teaching third graders in the Cecil Rhodes School. This was a disappointment.

She sighed, "In no time I seemed to be alone, and living in a different world."

Her college clique had scattered after commencement. As yet, she had not made new friends at the Vancouver Bible School, where she had begun attending some evening lectures. Then, too, for the first time in her life there was no parental roof to cover her head. Mr. and Mrs. Miller had sold their Vancouver home and moved to Victoria for Murray's sake as he had returned from World War I. So at that time Isobel was boarding in a private home. She made the ninth member of a lively household. Although they welcomed Isobel and begged her to join them, still she was not quite one of them. She felt lonely.

Besides, she was not happy teaching eight-year-olds. Bothered with discipline problems and bored with teaching elementary subjects, she began to fear failure. "This was to be my life work, but now I hated teaching. Needing help, I signed up for a teachers' convention in Seattle during some holidays."

As Isobel was leaving to take the Seattle steamer, a telegram was thrust in her hand. It was from her father. He informed her that he had arranged entertainment for her in the home of his Seattle friends, the Otis Whipples. Annoyed, Isobel resented this as interference with her fling at freedom. Did not she have plans of her own? Young life to see? Don, a former boy friend, too? How could Dad be so mean as to tie her down to some stuffy old religious friends of his?

But much as she wanted to, it was too late to telegraph Dad to cancel his plans, and mind his own business.

After her first day at the teachers' conference, Isobel had a dinner date and dance with Don. It was decidedly late when he escorted Isobel to the Otis Whipples' home. But Mrs. Whipple greeted her with a warmth of hospitality that relaxed the young teacher like an open fire on a hearth.

"Better and better I liked Mrs. Whipple. Instinctively, I knew that she was not one to barge into my inner sanctum without an invitation. So finally, when I was shown to my room, my porcupine quills were all safely laid flat."

That night Julia Whipple could not sleep for thinking of Isobel. Out of her bed, and down on her knees she went. "Why have You sent her to us, Lord? What is Your purpose and plan for this attractive girl? How can we help You to help her?"

The next day was Sunday. In the afternoon, on her own initiative, Isobel sought out her hostess; pouring into her sympathetic ears the baffling school-teaching troubles and disappointments. Then Mrs. Whipple, Spirit-led, felt she could speak plainly to the girl. "Isobel, it's like this: God has a plan for every life. The Bible says that He has created us unto good works, and *foreordained* that we should walk in them (Eph. 2:10). That means He has planned a useful life for you and He does so for each of us. The point as I see it is to find out God's will for your life and to follow it."

"How wonderful!" thought Isobel.

Somehow she did not remember hearing that before. She had only thought of God as a kind of fatherly Being, far off in the sky somewhere. "But," Isobel commented afterwards, "that He was minutely interested in *me*, had planned a career for *me*, just moved me deeply. Hardly able to control my voice, I asked, 'Well, how are we to find His plan for us?'

Mrs. Whipple reached for her Bible, and opening it before the kneeling girl, said, "Isobel, I've always found His will through His Word."

Then and there the Lord spoke to Isobel through the words of the Bible before her, and Mrs. Whipple beside her. The girl's faith looked up to God with new affection and a new sense of belonging to Him. It was a crisis in her life. Tears of great relief came in a stream. As God's own daughter, she now wholeheartedly began to seek His will for her future.

CHAPTER FOUR

BOUND BY A LOVE CHAIN

HOW thrilled Isobel Miller would have been that day could she have taken a long, long look into the past! She might have traced link after link in the love chain God forged to bind her to Himself.

More than a hundred years before this experience of Isobel's, there was a certain Christian mother in England. One day she had been so concerned for her restless teen-age boy, that she had relieved her anxiety by spending a day of prayer for him. That boy, Hudson Taylor, grew into a stalwart Christian statesman. By faith he founded the China Inland Mission by whose agency the good news of Christ was spread throughout China.

After his death, the story of Hudson Taylor and the China Inland Mission was written by his son and daughter-in-law, Dr. and Mrs. Howard Taylor. They worked twelve long years, and produced a spiritual classic, a two-volume biography. Supporting them while they worked was an American Christian business man.

The first volume of the story, with some other C.I.M. books, was tucked under the arm of a Mrs. Stott, a retired C.I.M. missionary, when one day she went out in the city of Vancouver, B.C., pushing door bells. She was longing to do something for Christ that day. And she did. She sold the first volume of Hudson Taylor's biography to Mrs. Otis Whipple.

Thoughtfully Julia and Otis Whipple read the inspiring story of *The Growth of a Soul*.[1] The result was that they eventually placed themselves and all their earthly possessions at God's disposal.

In July 1922, a few like-minded friends were invited by the Whipples to meet at "The Firs", their dedicated summer camp. Their purpose was to become better acquainted with Jesus Christ. Of course, no one could then foresee the way the Lake Whatcom

[1] First volume of Hudson Taylor's biography, by Dr. and Mrs. Howard Taylor, C.I.M.

Bible and Missionary Conference would grow from that beginning and would stretch out its hands in benediction to multiplied thousands over the world.

Julia Whipple's faith, prayers and her self-denying gift of money, managed to get Isobel to The Firs in July, 1923, to attend the second conference ever to be held there. Mrs. Whipple realized that the girl was quick, impulsive and impressionable, and that she needed Christian fellowship and grounding in God's Word lest an enemy "sow tares" in her life.

Isobel was one of the crowd in no time. She loved beautiful things, and there they were under a forest of firs near a large lake. She loved choice people. There they gathered, none finer. She loved study. There the Book of books was the text. She was beginning to love the Lord Jesus. The whole conference centred in Him.

Isobel remembered, "The leading spirit of us young people was Edna Whipple Gish, a young missionary, widowed in China by the tragic death of her husband. To Edna, it was given to lead me the next few steps of my way. I had often heard men of God give wonderful messages from the platform, but this was my first encounter with a Spirit-filled life in its daily commonplace habits. Edna and I slept in the same bed together, washed our faces in the same basin. I could watch her *off the platform*. It was Edna who taught me daily communion with God and holy habits.

"At the end of the week, when Edna pleaded with us to respond to Jesus' last request, 'Go ye into all the world and preach the gospel,' I raised my hand with the others. I had told Edna my story, and this offer to be a missionary was just a public expression of my covenant with God. My life was His."

(At that time Mrs. Gish could not possibly know how greatly God honoured her selfless persistence in speaking at those meetings, when the wounds of her widowhood were still so sore. But now, more than thirty years later, she sees that even through Isobel's one life, God's blessing has spread to unnumbered thousands.)

Isobel continued: "I had offered for the foreign field, but felt no particular call to any one field. When the conference ended, Mrs. Whipple lent me a book to take home, *The Growth of a*

Soul. It was that book which brought me further light as to God's plan for me. As I read how Hudson Taylor proved God; how he learned to move man, through God, by prayer alone, I was startled. That was what I was trying to do. And he had founded a missionary society on those principles—the China Inland Mission! I had gone to its prayer meetings when I was a child, not realizing what the Mission stood for. . . . A great longing to belong to that group came over me, that I might be linked with those who took God at His word, and daily proved Him a living and true God. I felt called to the Mission.

"Light regarding my life work was beginning to dawn, yet how unfit I was for it! I still danced, played cards and loved the theatre. I knew my father's religion frowned on such things, but I wasn't going to give them up just because of his attitude."

But after some further attempts at compromise, Isobel let these amusements go, one by one. Aptly she likened their attraction to candle light—no longer desired when the dawn brings the brightness of the sun. She felt that worldly society, indifferent or even hostile to Christ, was not for her any longer. She found she could not truly love Christ and the world at the same time. As she loved Him more she loved the world less; and as she loosened her hold on the world, she drew closer to Him.

It worked both ways.

Even back in her noisy boarding house, her loneliness found more than compensation in Christ's friendship. This became an intense joy as she determined to meet Him daily for an hour of prayer and Bible study. She selected two o'clock in the morning for the tryst. At that hour the house was quiet and her mind fresh. An increasing awareness of God's presence was the result. And no wonder the Father met with His eager young daughter!

Her spiritual life grew tremendously.

When July, 1924 came, she could hardly wait to rush off to the conference at The Firs.

CHAPTER FIVE

BLACK AND WHITE PEN SKETCH

"BEFORE she arrived everyone had been talking about her: often a poor way to set the stage for anyone. But I fell in love with her on sight. She went out to you, and that did it." So wrote a friend who first met Isobel that year at The Firs. "I have a memory of gaiety and much laughter. A black and white pen sketch would picture her well. Her complexion had not much colour. Her straight dark hair was fine and hard to hold in place. She was slim. A slight uptilt to her nose gave her quite a bit of piquancy. Her keen mind, her interest in the beauties of literature, her strong sense of responsibility in her family situation, these were other things I recall."

That summer Isobel worked as a waitress at the conference. She also began to take some leadership with the young people of the high-school age. One of these, now a mature Christian mother, writes, "I well remember Isobel's morning group meeting in the woods and the heart-searching messages she gave. One was based on Gareth and Lynette and the four gates. Another was woven around a string of pearls. Her talks were like her writing—vivid and appealing to young people. I also remember enjoying her rollicking sense of humour and quick wit, such wholesome balance it was. Her notes were kept in a small ruled notebook. . . . She had a precise way of keeping track of things." Another who was a high-schooler at that time remembers Isobel dreamily strumming her guitar and singing gospel songs and choruses.

"J. O. Fraser of Lisuland was there that summer," recalled another visitor, "and as he so graphically related his experiences among the Lisu in China it was very evident how Isobel took in all that he had to tell about those mountain tribespeople. On Saturday afternoon, at the end of the conference, we had an informal time of fun and entertainment. Isobel and her group realistically portrayed a party of Lisu welcoming their missionary on a mountain trail. The picture stands out in memory after all these years because of her dramatizing a scene which had become very real to her throughout the week."

From then on Tribesland became Isobel's definite goal and J. O. Fraser a lodestar of her life. Isobel could not forget those days. "Down in my seat on the side aisle I prayed, 'Lord I'd be willing to go . . . only I'm not a man.' Never did the vision of the Lisu tribe leave me. I dared not name this experience a 'call', but I believe that time has proved that it was."

Isobel also took on another life pattern that summer through J. O. Fraser's influence. "As I sat listening, I saw plainly how true it is that the Lisu church was born in prayer travail, and I decided that I must employ this weapon of 'all prayer' too."

Her whole life demonstrated her persistence in that decision.

Isobel's father enjoyed the conference with her that year. It was his invitation that drew J. O. Fraser to the Millers' home after ten days at The Firs. The great pioneer's presence and personal counsel gave Isobel a big lift when she really needed it.

She had a problem.

She knew she must go to Bible School before the China Inland Mission would consider her as a candidate. But she had been using her salary to pay off her college debts, and had no bank account. Her father could not help her. His rosy ideas about investments netted him only repeated business losses. Isobel started to pray definitely for funds to enable her to give up teaching and devote her whole time to Bible training.

Then something happened. It seemed to her like a miracle. Money fell into her lap through the God-guided hands of a mere acquaintance. Only her parents and one praying friend knew of Isobel's need, but indirectly Marjorie Harrison heard of it. Miss Harrison herself had been planning to go to China with the C.I.M. when she was turned back because of ill health. Now she presented her savings to Isobel, earmarked for transportation to Chicago and a year's tuition at Moody Bible Institute.

No wonder Isobel was overjoyed!

Then came a shock. As she shared this wonderful news with her parents, her mother's excited retort stunned her. Accept money from Marjorie? Why that was charity! . . . *Her* daughter live on charity? . . . A foreign missionary? Only those who could not find employment at home, or were disappointed in love, went to the foreign field! . . . Then dramatically Mrs. Miller shot out another flinty arrow.

"If you go to China it will be over my dead body. I'll never consent!"

Isobel sat staring at her mother aghast.

"My dear mother," she thought, "you first taught me to love the Lord Jesus. You've been president of the Women's Missionary Society in the Canadian Presbyterian Church for as long as I can remember. You have opened your home for C.I.M. prayer meetings. . . . My dear mother! Why are you now bitter because I feel called of God to be a missionary?"

Probably no one can ever answer that question with adequate understanding. Alice Miller loved her daughter. She also loved the Lord. Was it worry that was driving itself in like a wedge those days, a wedge between her and the Lord? If Mrs. Miller had not previously demonstrated that "God is our refuge and strength, a very present help in trouble," we might say that she had plenty to worry about just then. That year all Mr. Miller's savings, invested in two mining companies, had been lost. Besides, through a false accusation, he was threatened with a lawsuit. There was fear of a heavy fine being imposed or even a jail sentence. Murray, newly discharged from the army, was unemployed. Isobel explained, "That left only me as breadwinner, in case the judgement went against father. I was an 'ungrateful, conscienceless child' to go off and desert my mother at such a family crisis, she said. And so on and on, every day."

Stormy seas kept rocking the family boat. Each time the subject of missionary service churned the waves, Mrs. Miller was so upset that finally her husband forbad his daughter to speak another word about it. Sam Miller formerly had prayed that one of his children would become a missionary, but now Isobel felt he too was siding against her.

She was puzzled.

How was she to obey God's command to go into all the world and preach the gospel and still be obedient in the matter of honouring her father and mother?

It might have helped her had she known the fact that, as young feet start running towards the goal of the mission field, hindrances often loom up before them like high hurdles.

But the girl accepted God's challenge to her faith. She found in it her chance to

> "Move man
> through God
> by prayer alone."

With characteristic determination Isobel began jumping hurdles. Trunks were packed for Bible School, student visa procured, and the rail ticket was in hand. The last painful day arrived. But Mr. Miller still had to appear in court for trial.

"My boat was to leave at 2.30 p.m. and my father's case was not over until 10.30 a.m. I had to send my trunk to the boat, not knowing the outcome. You can imagine the tension of those last hours. At 10.30 our telephone rang. Daddy's voice came over the line. 'Praise God! Fully acquitted,' The Lord had vindicated my faith. So I left on the afternoon boat for Seattle, my mother's weeping face my last memory.

"It was a bitter experience for her to give up her only daughter and she was fighting it. That was not her norm. Mother was really a sweet generous woman. Her neighbours and friends would all testify to her unselfishness. I feel that I failed often to be as tender with her as was her due. I had yet to learn the suffering when one's affections are nailed to the cross. Little did I know that I was never to see Mother on earth again. Before 1924 was ended she was in heaven; all her tears wiped away forever. She died following an operation. Of course her words of prescience recurred to me and overwhelmed me with grief for a time.

"Later the Lord moved an old friend of Mother's to write me a long letter. This was the gist of it, 'The evening before your mother's operation she wrote to me saying that she was facing the morrow's serious surgery and in reviewing her life she had come to the conclusion that all her busy W.C.T.U. and Women's Missionary Society work had been but wood, hay and stubble. "I feel that my little girl has chosen the better part in wishing to devote all her life to the Lord." ' "

And from this clear token God showed Isobel that He had answered her prayers and that in due time she might proceed toward China having had her mother's full consent and blessing.

CHAPTER SIX

OUTSTANDING GIRL

IN Chicago a ruddy beaming face welcomed Isobel. It rose like the sun from the cloud of strange faces at the depot. Dr. Isaac Page, who had known Isobel since her childhood, grasped her suitcase and piloted her through traffic to Moody Bible Institute.

After her registration he took her for an ice-cream soda, eager to hear how the Lord had manœuvred her through the phase of college doubts and worldly allurements into new life objectives.

Nine years previously Isobel had been at the docks in Vancouver to wave Dr. and Mrs. Page away to China. At that time, when he had challenged her with "We're going to pray you out to the mission field, Isobel," she just retorted "How *mean* of you, Daddy Page!" Now as she told him how the Lord had been answering his patient prayers, tears of joy ran down his round cheeks.

For the first few months at the Institute gifts covered Isobel's expenses for board and room. But there were other needs; sharp winds snapped out a warning that a Chicago winter demanded warmer clothes than she had brought from Vancouver. And, to her dismay, she learned that first-term students were not allowed to supplement their funds by taking employment.

One day when Dr. Page was checking on how Isobel was getting on, she confided in him: "I'm not to work the first term. They say that's the ruling for everybody. I don't know yet what I'll do."

"We'll pray about it," was Isaac Page's only comment.

A couple of days later he sought her out. "I've got permission from the Dean to take you round the corner to introduce you to someone."

"Round the corner" led them to a bank and "someone" proved to be the bank's manager.

The introduction left Dr. Page one hundred dollars poorer

and Isobel with one hundred dollars in a newly-opened bank account. While she stammered her remonstrance her benefactor quieted her by saying, "Your father has given me as much as this and more in past years. This is just a small return to him —take it that way."

So Isobel thanked him but kept wondering how a poor C.I.M. missionary could find $100 to give away all of a sudden like that.

"Some twenty years later when, on a furlough, I met Dr. Page and decided to ask him, 'Was it a legacy?' He threw back his head and just laughed till he cried. 'No, Isobel,' he said, hilariously wiping the tears away, 'We just emptied our bank account, that was all. We figured that we were old-timers in the life of faith and you just a beginner. It would be easier for us than for you to trust the Lord. A legacy? Oh-ho-ho!' and off he went laughing again."

For several years Dr. Page was based at Chicago as regional secretary for the C.I.M. During Isobel's two years at the Institute she found him and his wife standing by her side in every emergency, counselling her, praying for her. And she was only one of hundreds they helped.

"She was the outstanding girl at Moody those days," said a woman who knew her there. And comments by another fellow-student fill out the picture. "In the autumn of 1925 Isobel was a Junior when I entered as a new student. I greatly admired her as she led our women's devotions or in the music for them in Massey Chapel. Isobel was not perfect; she was human and young. She had the faults which naturally accompanied her greater virtues. Whole-hearted and immediate in her own response to God herself, she did at times lack patience with weaker ones. She had a consuming zeal for their good and the glory of God, which occasionally lacked knowledge of the fact that the Holy Spirit had to be allowed time to do His work in a struggling soul. Once on a deputation assignment, when there was no response from a group of young people to the plea of the leader of the group for volunteers for foreign missionary service, Isobel impulsively darted to the front of the room and made such an impassioned and rebuking speech that one teen-ager, who had no call for such work and was really unfit for its spiritual and physical demands, went forward from sheer shame, responding to Isobel rather than to the Lord. Of course that was the end of this girl's missionary career!

"On another occasion she laid hold of a fellow-student who had volunteered for foreign missionary service and sought to compel her to attend a Saturday afternoon Student Volunteer meeting just about to begin. The girl hesitated. Isobel charged her with indecision in her own call, and with fear of letting her colours be known, whereas there were two factors in the situation of which Isobel was in ignorance. One was the fact that the girl had a high temperature and was on the way to the Infirmary, and the other was the fact that in the girl's home church a discerning pastor had warned his inner circle of young people against the modernism at that time creeping into the leadership of this movement, although of course the Moody Institute branch of it was sound. I know, because I was the girl in this case! The incident, though remembered, never affected my love for Isobel and our fellowship. Years later, when she was a mellow, mature and very wise teacher of young women, I asked her if she remembered thus 'nailing' me. She did not, of course, and was horrified at the thought.

"But at times, she had the wisdom of the Spirit far, far beyond her own years, far beyond the years of many a much older Christian. Watching her, I gained the impression which has never been altered: that Isobel walked habitually in a straight line—the straight and narrow line of the known will of God. Many of us circumnavigated in curves of ease or evasion or postponement of duty. Not Isobel. Therefore she had time and strength for a prodigious amount of work, good work, of all kinds; employment for financial needs—a heavy assignment as waitress at the big Montgomery Ward's cafeteria—sewing and grooming so that she always looked lovely; excellence in class work; a large amount of extra-curricular work on behalf of missions, deputation meetings, prayer meetings and personal friendships (which often, as in my case, amounted to a spiritual ministry)—with many of her schoolmates. She was instant and constant in obedience to her understanding of God's will; and that understanding was usually a safe guide, for she took time to be alone with God in His Word."

So Isobel's life had a wide intake and a full overflow.

Of the contributing streams of influence that poured into her receptive heart, Dr. Robert Hall Glover was one of the most important. As head of the Missions Course, he underlined certain principles to his students which Isobel practised from then on; "Keep mentally alert; read contemporary publications. Keep spiritually fit; feed on the best of spiritual books. Set aside time for reading every day." Probably much of Isobel's output as a writer could be traced to the source of good reading habits.

She remembered, too, Dr. Glover's emphasis on keeping up in personal appearance. This precept Isobel did not neglect even when she later was living far off among earth's humblest people. And in Chicago how it irked her to wear torn and ill-fitting uniforms when she dashed around as a rush-hour waitress in a large untidy lunch room! Things like this, hard and uncongenial, she allowed to work out death to her pride and impatience.

Pushing through difficulties or praying them out of the way was Isobel's chosen pattern. For instance, up came the problem of finding a whole hour each day to be alone with the Lord. That demanded some careful planning. Thirty minutes in the evening was not so hard—but that morning half-hour!

"At 6.30 a.m. I was due in the dining-room to set tables. I tried getting up at five but my health suffered. After various efforts I found I could maintain normal weight if I rose at 5.30. But where to get alone? My roommate slept through till nearly breakfast time and might be disturbed by a light at such an early hour. The only place I could find was the cleaning closet! So each morning I stole down the hall, turned the scrubbing pail upside down for a seat and in spite of mops and dust-rags, hanging around my head, I had a precious half-hour with the Master."

A friend noted that Isobel always seemed to have time to pray with others about their troubles, and that she was patient and forgiving, too, if anyone did not seem to appreciate her.

Appreciating Isobel, however, was not hard for most people. In fact, she was the popular choice of her senior class for their woman valedictorian.

And to top off all others who admired her, along came a stalwart young student, John B. Kuhn. He and his sister Kathryn were also pledged to the Lord for foreign service under the

C.I.M. Was it that factor that released the brakes in Isobel's mind and in due time shot John ahead of all others in her estimation?

Isobel tells the story of their first meeting in this way: "We met in the kitchen of the Moody Bible Institute at Chicago, in the year 1924. We were both students, having to work our way part, or wholly, through school. He had the job of running the dish-washing machine. I was, at that important moment, in the line of waitresses, waiting for the hot food to carry to the tables. It wanted but one minute for the bell to ring which would set us all in motion. I was a new student, burning with impatience to get through my training, so that I might be God's messenger to the Lisu tribe of the China-Burma border. So as I waited I thought disconsolately, 'Two years more of this before I can get there.'

"Quite unknown to me, the dish-washer had also gone into a day-dream, waiting for that bell to ring. He had one foot up on a chair, and with chin in his hand, he was dreaming out into space, unconscious that it was in the direction of the line of waitresses. As I turned quickly, I suddenly found myself falling down into the well of two blue, blue eyes. Down, down I went, until soul met soul, and the shock brought us to ourselves—both of us. Quickly each turned away and tried to get busy with something else; *but it had happened.* We had met, although I did not even know his name. It was three months before we were formally introduced, yet every day I had to pass him, in order to put away certain dishes. We never looked at one another nor spoke, yet somehow I was perfectly sure that Blue Eyes had investigated me, that he knew my name and all about me! And that was correct.

"I was slower to find out about him; he had come two terms before but as a new student I did not know how to make subtle inquiries! Eventually I was told that the man with the blue eyes was John Kuhn. It really did not matter what his name was, for from that first moment on, in my thinking it was HE—in capital letters.

"Gradually I discovered that we were both volunteers for China, and both interested in the China Inland Mission. The formality of introduction took place on Clark Street, one evening, while gathering for a surprise birthday party for Dr. Isaac Page. From then on, conversations in the kitchen at M.B.I. were proper, of course and the first request for a date took place while I was filling the evening teapot at the hot water urn!"

John and his pal Francis Fitzwilliam began double-dating Isobel and a friend of hers, Jennie. To boost their prospects, the boys invested in a second-hand car which they named "Jennybelle." Life at the Institute was not all hard work and serious meetings. Many a frolic did the two couples have bouncing along in good old Jennybelle!

But the course of true love for John Kuhn and Isobel Miller had its ups and downs too. After all, John was four years Isobel's junior, came from sturdy Pennsylvania-Dutch stock, and was quite the temperamental opposite of Irish-Canadian Isobel. Something happened to make the girl doubt that a future union of their lives was in the directive will of God. Yet she did not pour maudlin tales into the romance-hungry ears of her girl friends. Even one who was of her inner circle knew only that she and John were no longer seen together and that Isobel was suffering because of the separation. The onlooker noticed, "She went straight on with the Lord. As a daughter of the King she didn't cheapen any phase of her life, especially its very core, by indulging in self-pity or self-revelation."

Was this the same young woman who had petulantly thought of taking her life when broken-hearted over her first love affair? How differently she reacts from a few years before! Now, with the Lord first in her affections, He steadies her, as she grasps His almighty arm. Now she finds stability—the real kind, that He offers to everyone of His own in every time of need!

"And there wasn't even an understanding between us," Isobel confessed, "when John finished his course at the Moody Bible Institute and sailed for China in the autumn of 1926."

CHAPTER SEVEN

ACROSS A WIDE OCEAN

HOW large the Pacific seemed!
To bridge that wide, wide expanse of salty water, John on one side of it and Isobel on the other, they began to communicate.

Letters crept along. Thoughts flew. Prayers ascended.

Meanwhile Isobel was graduated from the Bible Institute. That was in December, 1926, around Isobel's twenty-fifth birthday. Next, as a candidate for the China Inland Mission, she went to the Toronto home. Then came a long wait, while the anti-foreign uprisings of 1927 burned like bonfires in China. The conflagration necessitated a withdrawal of C.I.M. workers from inland China and concentrated them at Shanghai. Besides, it hindered new workers from setting out from America and Great Britain.

What a frustrating situation for a high-spirited girl like Isobel Miller!

And another fiery trial blazed up, threatening to block her path to China. One of her six references instead of recommending her to the C.I.M. Council came out with some disqualifying charges against her. Looking around for a sympathetic hearing for her troubles, she broke the story to a student she had known at Bible School. But his response came as a shock. "Isobel," he wrote, "what amazes me most is your attitude. You sound bitter and resentful. Why, if anyone said to me 'Roy, you are proud, disobedient, and a trouble-maker,' I would admit, 'Amen! brother! and even then you haven't said the half.' "

Roy had used the ugly words "bitterness and resentment." The words cut for a moment, but Isobel met their challenge. "After all," she thought, "bitterness and resentment are as serious sins as pride, disobedience, and trouble-making."

At once she dropped down on her knees, convicted and confessing. She was not one to sit around moping when she knew something must be set right with the Lord. It made her too unbearably miserable. Then when the Holy Spirit assured her of God's forgiveness, she got to her feet, humbled but happy again.

Months later when she stumbled on the identity of the referee who had written to her detriment, Isobel easily accounted for the reason why that person had criticized her. Should she justify herself by exposing the bias she felt sure existed?

"No," she thought, "Why try to make the Mission think I'm lily-white? They'll have personal experience before long as to just how earthly a person I am." Then afterward she explained, "You see, the Lord foreknew there was a work to be done in Vancouver before I sailed for China; and my self-confidence needed to be thoroughly jarred before He dared put this delicate work into my hands. That experience of His enfolding love has blessed me all my life."

Back home in Vancouver, Isobel spent most of 1927 and 1928 keeping house for her father and brother while she also built up a thriving work for God as superintendent of the Vancouver Girls' Corner Club.

There she more than demonstrated her qualifications for the foreign mission field. When doors to China again opened, she was heartily accepted, "unconditionally and unanimously," as a member of the China Inland Mission.

During most of the years as superintendent of the Corner Club Isobel, like a magnet, winsomely drew to the Lord high-school and business girls. "It was thrilling," wrote one of the girls, "to hear Isobel's hearty laugh; challenging to hear her gospel messages; inspiring to hear her pray, and humbling to know that a life so yielded to the Lord was being lived in the midst of girls from all walks of life in needy Vancouver. Isobel was a young woman in whose presence you felt right at home. But you could realize without any question that no unseemly liberties were permitted, no gossip, no petty talk, no harsh judgement of others. It was mainly through Isobel's influence that Bible School training became a reality for me, for she seemed to know her Bible so well, trusted its promises so implicitly and knew its Author so intimately that I, too, craved a deeper acquaintance with God and His Word. It is to her credit to say that she did not encourage girls to place confidence in *her*, but to put their trust in the Lord."

This is illustrated by another girl who recalls going to Club on a certain blue day. "I saw Isobel there and went in. I hadn't been feeling well and my work at the office seemed too much. Isobel saw that something was wrong and asked me what was the matter. After a few words of prayer together, she held out the Promise Box to me, and said, 'Take a promise, May.' I did, and found it was 2 Corinthians 12:9 'My grace is sufficient for thee, for my strength is made perfect in weakness.' She said to me, 'Don't you see, May, *is*, is present tense—right now! You can go back to the office on that promise.' I did, claiming it as I had never done before, leaning harder on the Lord moment by moment through that day, proving afresh God's unfailing supply."

Isobel's insight into human nature, her sense of humour and dramatic gift soon spotlighted her as an able public speaker. She selected and trained a quartet of girls who teamed up with her when she was asked to speak to local church groups. Of course at the Club she constantly used her natural gifts (no less God-given than the spiritual gifts). Sometimes on recreation night she "brought down the house" playing around in a character part.

Believing that young life must have an outlet, Isobel planned picnics, seaside corn-roasts, hikes on Saturday afternoons, and in the winter, a Stunt Night—girls only. "Most of them had never seen me lay aside the dignity of my office just for fun, and it tickled their fancy to find I could enjoy a joke as much as the next one. That Stunt Night broke the ice between me and a certain girl for whom I had been fishing in vain for weeks. It was only a short time afterwards, that she accepted the Lord in my office. All our parties were threaded through with the love of the Lord and a deep earnestness that others might find Him too. . . . I think that is the secret, for a merely social club helps nobody very much, since it doesn't offer any real solution to the basic problems of life."

One of the "girls"—now a mature woman—well remembers the day she met Isobel for the first time. "I had changed my position, and found myself working in a very difficult place. I was worn out, unhappy and dissatisfied. In this frame of mind I took myself up to the Club—just another Tuesday meeting! In the lounge where we assembled before going into the dining-room a dear friend of mine came over to me and, catching my hand said, 'Come quickly and meet the new superintendent.' I shall never forget my surprise. Could this lovely, tall, slim girl with the friendly smile and charming manner actually be our new superintendent! She was young—only in her twenties, and bound for China (What a shame! I thought.) Another day at noon I wandered up to the Corner Club. Isobel was in her office and we had a chat about the Lord. Then we prayed together. I rose from my knees a new creature in Christ Jesus. She had asked me to pray, too, which I did although shyly. I remember how she put her arms around me. An intense, loving nature, warm and affectionate! How I have thanked God for her life!"

Scores of other Corner Club girls would still say Amen to that testimony even though more than thirty years have passed since Isobel waved them all goodbye at the Vancouver wharf.

"Isobel based her farewell message to the Club on Hebrews 6:1 'Let us go on,'" wrote one of the Club members. "After seeing her sail away six of us ran up the ramp, our hearts just full. We hurried directly to the telegraph office to send her a telegram on board ship. 'We will go on!' and signed our names. Deep down was the earnest desire to accept her challenge to live for Christ."

Very evidently many inspired by Isobel at the Corner Club did just that—they went on with God. They can be found today standing as sincere Christians, true to their purpose; and besides, several of them have kept right on praying for the mission work, and the individuals that she taught them to love.

Now, with three decades of perspective, how our foggy understanding clears! And we see how the Lord used the two short years of trial and delay to enrich Isobel's life as well as to bless innumerable other lives through hers.

It was on October 11, 1928, that she eventually sailed for China. She was not quite twenty-seven years old.

By that time John Kuhn had had two years in the Orient and a big start in the language and in field experience. Meanwhile significant letters had kept floating from China to Canada—and from Canada to China. And, after all, it is a fact that Isobel Miller was a *ready writer* and that John Kuhn was a *good correspondent*.

How *ready*? And how *good*?

Well, anyone in the large crowd of Isobel's friends waving

her away at the ship could see that she was proudly wearing an engagement ring!

After she had reached China Isobel was the subject of an ecstatic letter John wrote to one who had been like a mother to him from his boyhood. (And while he described his fiancée he revealed himself in the writing, quite unconsciously.)

"I constantly in my thoughts and prayers kept her on the altar. There was none other with whom I could have more perfect Christian fellowship. Yet, unless the Lord Himself was kept supreme in the matter, I should not have felt that I had received His guidance and had followed out His will. Thank God! We were both led in the same way and God has given wonderful joy and peace in our decision. Her experience in the school of suffering far surpasses any little that I've ever had. I admire this so much in her. Then her natural gifts are so rich. As a public speaker she is intense and holds attention, using a different style from most women. She plays the piano very nicely and sings, and also plays the guitar. Her attainments include an arts degree from the University of British Columbia, Normal School, besides a year or so of teaching, and then two or more years at Moody (Bible Institute). There are indeed no qualities lacking. Yet, if she had not been exceptional in her life and service for God, all these gifts and graces put together would not have drawn me. You may rejoice with me in that she knows Calvary and its victory, and *her desire is only Christ and Him alone.*"

Part Two

THE VISION PURSUED

PART TWO

THE VISION PURSUED

SEVERAL of the next years of Isobel Kuhn's life she spanned in an unpublished manuscript. In her own frank and graphic style she revealed an unusually intimate side of her life as a young missionary. Here are incidents a biographer would hardly presume to tell. They reveal the little-apprehended fact that God does not wait to find perfection before He uses a person, or He could never use any one of us. Rather, as a Father, He perfects while He employs His children. How He did this for Isobel Kuhn she relates in the following chapters. Somewhat abridged, we use her *Vistas* as PART TWO of this biography.—C.C.

"When I was laid aside with sickness in 1954, friends suggested that I write down some memories. The most valuable ones were jotted down first, but as days were still given me, the whimsical thought came to open up some vistas which I had glimpsed one morning long ago in far-off Lisuland."

ISOBEL KUHN

CHAPTER ONE

ANTICIPATION

AFTER I was accepted by the China Inland Mission, John Kuhn's letters began to have a personal note which meant only one thing. But I had a question. I felt called to the Lisu tribe of Yunnan province, and John had been somewhat interested in the far northwest of Kansu—the opposite direction. So I wrote to John's sister, Kathryn Kuhn Harrison, telling her to warn him not to propose until he had been designated! My letter crossed one from him on the ocean. Designations had taken place earlier than expected, and he was assigned to *the tribes of Yunnan*! And would I be his wife and go with him? He asked me to cable the answer. Cable *Light* if I accepted him, *Dark* if I refused.

There was no question in my mind as to what my answer was, yet as I spread that precious letter out before the Lord there was still a problem. John and I are of very opposite dispositions, and each likewise is rather strong minded. Now, Science has never discovered what happens when the Irresistible Force collides with the Immovable Object. Whatever would happen *if they married one another*? "Lord, it must occur sooner or later. Art Thou sufficient for even that?" The verse He gave me was Matthew 6:33, "*Seek ye first the kingdom of God, and His righteousness; and all these things shall be added unto you.*"

So I cabled back *Light*, and then wrote a letter suggesting that our marriage motto might be: *God first*. The cable was directed to Shanghai Headquarters but John had to be sent for, as he was living in a house some distance away. When he read the word *Light* he was so transported with joy that, getting on the street car to return home, he dreamily sailed right past the conductor, forgetting such a small earthly matter as paying one's fare! The conductor, however, being well rooted in the earth, gave a grunt and went after him in pursuit. The grins of fellow travellers brought John somewhat to his senses!

We were to be married in Kunming, the capital city of Yunnan province. John was stationed down the railway line at a little town named Chengchiang. I was studying the language in Kunming. Originally we had planned on November 14, 1929, for our wedding day, but suddenly had to change it to November 4. The American Consul had an unexpected call to leave the city and could not be present if we retained the later date. Hastily I sent a runner to Chengchiang to ask if John could make the earlier day. He brought the answer by coming himself— such an exciting arrival! Tongues flew as we discussed new arrangements, until the ring was mentioned. "Oh," cried my bridegroom, "didn't I go and forget the wedding ring! I left it in its box in Chengchiang!" Well, in that big city we could borrow a substitute and we were not superstitious, so it was all right.

But even that oversight was corrected. Chu Yin-chang, the young Chinese who was John's cook, companion and "boy" arrived the next day, and—the wedding ring with him! After John left, Yin-chang had been going through his drawers and found the little box; knowing what it was, he had brought it along. John had always been loud in the praises of his wonderful cook, and now the encomiums soared sky high. It never occurred to either of us to ask what he was doing going through his master's bureau drawers after that said master had left—the world was all rosy and everyone in it a contributor to our joy.

That evening we went for a walk outside the city gate, where there were stretches of rice fields and not many pedestrians.

"Just think, dear," I said beaming, "this time next week we will be married!"

"Ye-es," answered my dearly beloved, but in such a gloomy voice that I cast him a startled look. "Yes, we will have been married. *And then there will be nothing to look forward to!*"

Anticipation! It had tasted so sweet he was reluctant to see it slip away! After all, there is something to be said for anticipation. It does have its own special delight, never again to be exactly reproduced.

CHAPTER TWO

GETTING MARRIED IS NOT A PRIVATE AFFAIR AFTER ALL

IN Kunming, provincial capital of Yunnan, the China Inland Mission had two houses. One was the Guest House and business centre, which served all our missionaries in the province. The other was the home of the missionary couple who supervised the work in the local church, and in the many outstations which had been established in country towns within a wide radius around the city. John was staying at the Guest House and I was with the church workers, and the hostess at each place took a keen interest in our wedding. Let us call them Mrs. A and Mrs. B.

Mrs. A was the ascetic type who felt that missionaries should live with the nationals and be as self-denying as possible. Mrs. B who was in charge of the Guest House, had a distinct gift for arranging her home in an attractive style, and did not feel it wrong to spend a little money to maintain it thus. As many of our Yunnan workers lived in the mountains among the tribes where life was primitive and hard, she felt that, on the few occasions which brought them out to civilization for medical or dental treatment, they should have comfortable rooms and good food. It is obvious that two such opposite opinions of missionary living would not always agree.

Now my own idea of a wedding was of an occasion so sacred that one would not wish many onlookers. By nature I am the solitaire who does not enjoy crowds. I had also to learn that John was my opposite in this, and that, to him, the more people there were around the more joy it gave him. However, men are usually shy on their wedding day, and he was with me in wanting only a few people to be present when we exchanged our vows before the Lord.

It was customary for the hostess at the Guest House to assume the responsibility of entertainment in lieu of the bride's mother, so we proceeded to confide in Mrs. B our wish that only a select few be present.

Now in some of these Far Eastern countries the white community does not often have reason for a celebration together, so a wedding is regarded as a social affair. I had noted a peculiar expression pass over Mrs. B's face when I first intimated that we did not wish a crowd at our wedding, but she kindly repressed her own sentiments and left me none the wiser. Shopping one day, however, I was stopped by a lady of another mission. She was a sympathetic, motherly soul and gave my hand a warm squeeze. "My dear," she said, "I hear that you are to be married! Well, I just love weddings. You won't mind if I just slip into the back seat and look on, will you? I don't want anything to eat, you understand!" This last was added hurriedly, much to my amusement. It was obvious now that she was thinking our plans for such a small affair might have a financial reason! I could not be blunt and say, "It's because I don't want half-strangers at such a sacred moment." There was nothing to do but to invite warm-hearted Mrs. X to come. So I asked Mrs. B to prepare for one more. Again there came that quizzical smile, but nothing was said, and I went blissfully on.

But the next day another lady stopped me on the street, and asked to come in on that back bench at our wedding! And she also was profuse in her assurance that she did not need anything to eat! I invited her, too. What else could one do?

When I reported *this* to Mrs. B she looked anxious. "Miss Miller," she said, "I do not see how you can possibly invite Mrs. X and Mrs. Z and leave out Mrs. Y. Mrs. Y is an old friend of the Mission. She would never dream of giving a wedding and not inviting me, for instance. And Mrs. X is a comparative new-comer. And if Mrs. W heard that X, Y, and Z were invited and she left out! Dear me, I am sorry, but I do not know where you are going to draw the line. I do hope this wedding of yours will not cause ill feelings." And she looked at me anxiously. After the wedding we would be going to our station and would seldom see these people again, but Mrs. B must continue to live among them. We saw the point and, to cut a long story short, we ended up with the inevitable—all the Westerners of Kunming were invited.

But this was not the end of our problems. One evening, some days before the wedding, my hostess Mrs. A appeared at the supper table looking rather fatigued but triumphant.

"I've been all day working over at the Peng Gardens, getting some rooms ready for you and John to occupy for your honeymoon," she announced. "There is no reason why you should spend money going across the lake, when the C.I.M. still has a lease on that place. You have Yin-chang and his bride to cook for you, and you will have a lovely time right among the Chinese." It sounded reasonable and I was quite overwhelmed with her kindness in labouring so for us. I was not slow to tell Mrs. B of this unexpected graciousness. But I was quite unprepared for Mrs. B's reaction.

"Oh, but you *can't* do that!" she almost wailed. "I've arranged for you to rent the honeymoon cottage across the lake. It does not cost much for a week. I meant to send your meals over to you by boat, so you would be quite alone with all those lovely walks and the climb to the temple and the Chinese village to visit. Peng's Gardens? And Yin-chang to cook for you! Why, he and his wife would watch everything you did—with the Peng family to aid them. A honeymoon comes only once in a lifetime. Oh, I do hope you won't feel you have to accept just because Mrs. A spent a morning cleaning the place up!" It was easy to see that Mrs. B was distressed over the matter. At the same time Mrs. A was quite taking it for granted that we were going to Peng Gardens, and telling people so. John and I retired for consultation.

"Well, let's go to Peng Gardens," said John, "Since Mrs. A has gone to such trouble, and it is true we would have Yin-chang to do the cooking for us."

"But Mrs. B has brought out a point that we were too inexperienced to foresee for ourselves," I replied thoughtfully. "If I remember rightly you yourself have been telling me that in Chinese eyes, the chaste and high-minded newlyweds observe the greatest indifference to one another in public. They are never seen to speak to one another until the first child is born—didn't you say that? And they never call each other by their first names; the bride refers to him as *the person outside the house* and the groom refers to her as *the person inside the house*. When we begin to live among the Chinese we must be careful to conform to their ideas in this manner, but I certainly hope I can have at least one week when I may treat you and be treated normally. And just think how curious the Pengs and Yin-chang would be; we would be watched every moment."

"Well, that is true. So then we'd better decide to go across the lake, eh!"

"That would be ideal, as Mrs. B advised. But seeing that feeling is running rather warm between the two, as to whose advice we are to take, I think the most important matter is not where to go, but how we can avoid resentment between Mrs. A and Mrs. B over the matter. After all, we will be leaving here and seldom returning. But they must continue to live just around the corner from one another ad infinitum. I would prefer that they both be disgusted with *us*, rather than that anything resembling a root of bitterness spring up between them. Is it necessary to have a honeymoon at all? Can we not go right off to our station!"

"No, we can't do that. There's no night train. We've got to spend our wedding night somewhere near here. There's no town where we get off the train and no place to hire coolies for our luggage and your mountain chair. I've already arranged that such coolies come over the mountain from Chengchiang and meet a certain train on a certain day. We have to make that connection or we'll be in a pickle for sure."

"Well, what can we do?" we thought and thought.

"Is there no third place we can go for a honeymoon, dear?" I asked at length. "You've been here for other weddings!"

"Yes," John said, "most missionaries go across the lake to that cottage Mrs. B is talking about. But there is a French hotel, you know. Business people sometimes go there, I believe. But my, that costs!"

The French hotel was run on European lines by a European manager and mainly catered to the French population of Kunming who, being officials in the Salt Gabelle or other industries, were usually well-to-do people. But the arrival of the mail from America brought a deciding factor. There was a letter from John's father in which he enclosed a substantial cheque as a wedding gift for us!

"Here we are, Belle!" John cried, grinning and waving that

important piece of slim paper. "Here is enough for a week's honeymoon at the French hotel!"

"Good," I made answer, "Dear Daddy Kuhn, bless his heart! Mrs. B will be as horrified at our extravagance as Mrs. A. But it is not misusing any money given for Mission purposes. It has absolutely no tags on it. We'll let Daddy Kuhn give us our honeymoon." And so it was settled.

The news of our decision caused both Mrs. A and Mrs. B to throw up their hands in dismay, as we had foreseen; but this unexpected unity of opinion paved the way for doing the best they could for such reckless youngsters who had yet to learn C.I.M. economies.

I always thought that our wedding was the most beautiful of any that I ever saw. We were married in the Chinese church, and the good ladies had transformed it until the whole looked like a lawn party in the woods! It was a completely happy day.

As we rode off in rickshas for the French hotel, we turned to wave to our group of friends. And there were our two dear hostesses, standing in unconscious union, trying to wave hopefully to us, but each dubiously shaking her head over those unmanageable and extravagant Kuhns!

CHAPTER THREE

OUR FIRST HOME—WHAT COMES FIRST?

HONEYMOON over, we set out for our station in the town of Chengchiang. Yin-chang, John's serving boy, but recently married himself, had gone on ahead to get things ready for us.

We travelled down the French Railway until about noon, when we came to the spot where we were to proceed overland. Porters to carry our things and a mountain chair for me were already waiting there for us. John chose to walk. It was a beautiful trip over high velvety wrinkled mountain ranges, piled up one against another to the skyline, affording deep glimpses into separating valleys where quaint little hamlets lay.

But it had rained for many days previously and the mountain trails were slippery. My coolies had to pick their steps so carefully that time was lost, and the sun set before we were two-thirds of the way. For an hour and a half we had to feel for our path, with constant danger of a false step and broken bones. And the last half-hour the porters dared carry me no further, so down I got. Dusk was falling, so I could not see the way plainly, and, with John holding one arm and a Chinese coolie the other, we slid, jumped, and ran down the last slopes on to the plain.

Just as we reached the level, the moon came out and flooded all objects in soft white light. On three sides towered dark shadowy masses—the surrounding mountains. Far off, on the fourth side, at the end of the plain, gleamed a silver sheet of water, a lake. I was so thrilled with the beauty that I sent up a Thank You through the starlit sky to the Giver of every good gift.

But we still had to cross the plain. A shout ahead—and a lighted lantern approached us—it was one of the Chengchiang Christians come out in search of the missing bride and groom.

"Courage, Belle," said my dear John to very weary me. "He says that Yin-chang has a lovely Chinese feast waiting for us—

been waiting for hours as I usually get in before dark when I make this trip," and so we plodded on. At length a great wall of mud and two huge massive doors loomed up before us.

"Chengchiang city-gate, Belle dear. They close it at 6 o'clock, but Mr. Yang told them we were coming and the watchman has orders to open for us. Not much farther now." But I was speechless with weariness and could only stumble over the rough cobblestones of the streets until we reached a certain doorway.

"Here we are, Belle!" John called out excitedly. "Welcome home!" And as he spoke he stooped, picked me up, and carried me over the threshold and up the stairs. "This is *our home*! Want to see it?"

"Oh, not tonight, dear. Just give me a bed," was all I could get out, completely exhausted and faint, as we had not eaten for many hours.

"Aren't you going to come down to supper? Yin-chang has cooked such a big meal!"

But I was at the end; words took too much strength. I just shook my head. "Bed" was merely boards on a trestle with a mattress on top, but to stretch out and be still was pure luxury.

"Isn't there anything you can eat?" inquired my bridegroom anxiously. I thought a moment. "Hot soup?"

"Yes. I've got a tin, I think. Just a minute," and he was gone. Shortly he was back with a big bowl of steaming hot tomato soup. Oh, was it good! It tasted like nectar—my first meal in our own home.

The next morning I was thoroughly renewed and as keen to inspect the premises as John was to escort me around.

"I told you it wasn't much," John kept saying anxiously. And it wasn't. Two rooms over a little chapel, and right on the market street. There were no windows at all, but the front and back walls were folding doors which could be rolled back in the daytime. If you rolled them back, you got the light but no privacy. Anyone walking down the street could look right up and see in. If we wished privacy we had to shut the doors and go into the semi-light of a closed wooden box—there was no electricity, of course. The Oriental cannot understand the Westerner's desire for privacy. Dishonest and evil deeds need to be kept out of sight, of course, but why anything else? What do you contemplate doing that the public should not view it?

An upper back veranda, at the head of which a native stove had been built, was the kitchen. And in the side wing of the house were two small dark rooms where Yin-chang and his bride lived. The house was owned by Chinese Muslims who were still living in the back wing. To do our laundry we had to take our zinc tubs and clothes and go through the Muslims' home to the back garden where there was a well. After washing, our clothes had to be hung on our own upper and side verandas. Anything that was not securely fastened and which happened to blow down over the railing was seized by those below as their lawful prey. I saw them using a handkerchief or towel of ours from time to time, so I was able to guess where the wind had carried our missing things!

But I was not dismayed at our poor quarters. I knew the C.I.M. sent their missionaries to live right among the people, and I was prepared for anything. I did not mind living in a humble place for the Lord's sake, but I saw no reason why I should not make it as *attractive* as possible. So I had come prepared with enamel paint and cretonne.

It is true that Mr. Hoste, our General Director, had said something about this in my first personal interview with him. I really had not understood what made him say it; but he had said, "Miss Miller, if I had a beautiful bedspread, I would throw it in the river." I was startled. Did he have X-ray eyes! I *did* have a beautiful quilt in my boxes, a wedding gift from a girl friend. But however did Mr. Hoste know that? And if he did, why should he object? I murmured politely, "Is that so!" or some such filler-in, but inwardly I had answered, "Well, I'm not throwing *my* quilt into the river!" It was a lovely thing—would trim up a shack very nicely, you know.

This windowless, wooden upstairs was an agreeable challenge. With wedding gift money we had bought some pretty rattan furniture. As a bachelor John had lived on backless benches, but now we had a small settee, a couple of chairs, a table and a rattan rug, all in natural tones. The uneven, warped floor boards disappeared under the rug. In one corner I had to put my big trunk—there was no other place for it—but I had a pretty green and crimson travelling rug which I pinned over it as a cover. John's table-desk (off which we ate) was in another corner, and soon the dull room had blossomed into a nice living-room.

When the bedroom had been fixed up in blue and white, the place was really transformed. And so began our life among the country Chinese people.

Already there was a small church in Chengchiang and there I was introduced by John. I was proud of his fluent Chinese and glad that one of us, at least, could speak and understand. Truly we were living right among the people. We had come for them, and they were not long in coming to us.

"Visitors, Belle!" John called out one afternoon, and a busy chatter of voices ascending the stairs brought me running. A group of peasant women who had come to market were to be my first lot of heathen guests. Delightedly I welcomed them and showed them into our pretty brown and green sitting-room. They admired it very much and I was glad to share it with them —or thought I was. After they were seated I began to explain the gospel message, as much as my one year and four months of language study allowed. I was thrilled to see that they understood me.

We were getting along fine when, all of a sudden, an oldish woman who was sitting on my big trunk in the corner, blew her nose with her fingers, and—*wiped the stuff off on my beautiful travelling rug*! In another minute a young mother laughingly held her baby son out over my new rattan rug. She carried him to the door, but as she went she carefully held him out over the rug so that a wet streak ran down the centre of my cherished floor covering. Since their own floors were of earth my visitor had no idea that she was doing anything offensive to me. That was just their custom.

Outwardly I managed to remain courteous, escorted them to the door when they rose to leave, and in time-honoured Chinese fashion begged them to go slowly and come again. Then I returned to my deflated sitting-room and stood looking at it— that disgusting gob on my travelling rug, and the discoloured streak across the pretty new mat. Hot resentment rose in my heart, and then there followed my first battle over *things*.

Suddenly I understood what Mr. Hoste had meant. "Miss

Miller, if I had a beautiful bedspread, I would throw it into the river." He did not mean that he did not like beautiful things. He meant that if possessions would in any way interfere with our hospitality, it would be better to consign them to the river. In other words, if your finery hinders your testimony throw it out. In our Lord's own words, *if thine hand offend thee, cut it off*; He was not against our possessing hands, but against our using them to hold on to sinful or hindering things.

So I faced my choice. In our first home—what was to come first? An attractive sitting-room just for ourselves? Or a room suited to share with the local Chinese?

Our engagement motto hung silently on the wall—*God first*. Mentally I offered that pretty rattan furniture to the Lord to be wrecked by the country peasants if they chose. The day was not far off when we were called to leave Chengchiang and move west to Tali. Then I had an opportunity to begin anew. I sold that rug and the rattan furniture to the Chinese postmaster's wife, and our Tali guest hall was plainly furnished with the local wooden lacquer chairs and tea tables, which could be easily washed and were such as all the Chinese had.

CHAPTER FOUR

HOW TO DEVELOP A TASTE FOR BEANCURD

IT had been agreed between us that for the first five months after our marriage John should run the housekeeping, with the help of his cook-boy, Yin-chang. There were good reasons for starting out in this topsy-turvy way:

The China Inland Mission requires that missionaries be two years on the field before uniting in marriage. This rule has been called in question from time to time, and it just had happened that we struck a period when the Mission revoked the two-year rule in favour of a trial of one year. Later they returned to the two-year rule, believing in it more firmly than ever. But John and I came in on this one-year trial period and decided to take advantage of it. By this time, of course, John had been in China three years, but our superintendent, Mr. J. O. Fraser, was disappointed. "I had hoped," he said, "that you two would set an example and wait the two years anyway. Now Miss Miller will never get the language well."

If his wife's freedom to study Chinese was all that was against our marrying at the end of one year, John cheerfully offered to run the household until my third language examination was finished. He had run it in his bachelor days, so it would merely be continuing with his old routine. And with wonderful Yin-chang as cook, we anticipated no problems. (As a matter of fact I did get my language exams written off in less than the allotted period, despite Mr. Fraser's prophecy.) Our real reason for desiring an early marriage was to release me for country work and witness. Brigandage abounded in the country areas those days. Kunming had been besieged by a powerful brigand and all the single ladies had been quickly called in from the outer parts, and word was given that only married women with their husbands would be allowed to work outside the city gates. There seemed no prospect of the situation clearing soon and, as workers within the walls were many and those in the country places pitifully few, we felt we had the Lord's permission to marry and go to these needy ones. So we got married.

Good servants were scarce in Yunnan. I remember that as far back as our language school days, our principal, Mrs. Alice Macfarlane, had counselled us to begin to pray for domestic help. I had told her proudly of Yin-chang, and how fortunate I was that I would not have the servant worries such as young brides often had. She did not say much in reply, but gave me a quizzical look, for which I could not account at the moment, but remembered with *understanding* later.

Our days were well filled. Early every morning John held a Bible class for the converts, of which the Lord had given us a fine group. An ex-actor, Mr. Yang, had been brought to Christ largely through John's witness, also a Taoist priest named Deng, and a slave girl and others. All morning I studied the language, John also having some time with the teacher; there was street chapel in which he preached and I played the folding organ. In the afternoons we often went into the villages on the plain outside the city gate. Souls were won to Christ those days who remained true to Him through later years of testing.

It was John who suggested our first trip afield together.

Some months before our marriage, he and Tom Mulholland had heard of another valley-plain about seventeen miles from Chengchiang called Yangtsung. They had paid a quick visit to it before going to Kunming for our wedding, but no one had been there since. They found a farming population with about twenty villages, and as far as we know, no white man had ever been there before. The gospel message was absolutely new to them. John now proposed that we make up an evangelistic party and give a week's preaching to Yangtsung and plain. Yin-chang and his bride would go with us, and one of the recent men converts (I think it was actor Yang) to add his testimony to ours.

"This is what I've long looked forward to doing, darling," said John, "to lead you over the beautiful hills of Yunnan!" And in truth the joy of those treks for Him, with Him, and with one another, continued to highlight our married life for many years.

Arriving on Yangtsung plain we went to the market town. There was no hotel in such a small place, so they sent us to an old temple where we could sleep in an upstairs room, and Yin-chang could cook for us downstairs. I was the first white woman those Chinese had ever seen, and they simply thronged us day and night. We could not eat or sleep without an audience. Boys climbed the temple walls and appeared at our window. Others climbed neighbouring roofs to look in and watch. Exhausted after being on display from morning to night, I would go to bed, only to have women request that they might come up and talk to me while I was in bed! I would preach my one little sermon and then John or Mr. Yang would give them a good talk on the way of salvation.

During the day we went on to the plain, preaching from village to village; but each evening we held an open air meeting in Yangtsung market, where our temple-inn was. I had my Hawaiian guitar along and I chorded as we sang choruses and sacred songs in Chinese. One evening as I was accompanying the singing, I looked up to find our little group at the bottom of what seemed a cone of eager, living, yellow faces! The Chinese had climbed on benches, window sills, roofs, anywhere they could, to watch the guitar. As I looked up at them, all I could see in any direction were Chinese—Chinese—Chinese; until immediately overhead my eyes at last met the tranquil beauty of the dark, star-spangled sky. Oh, what deep joy thrilled my heart! All these were listening to the old, old story—many for the very first time.

By the end of that week's effort, a little group of inquirers had been called out for the Lord.

Yin-chang and his wife had nothing to do all day except cook our meals, but as we ate Chinese food with them, that was no arduous task. But meal after meal there appeared only rice and beancurd; maybe some meat but always beancurd. Soya beancurd. It tasted to me like squares of flannel boiled, or scorched flannel fried. At first I thought maybe that small town produced nothing else, but as I went out early and looked I saw a lovely variety of potatoes, carrots, onions, cabbage—indeed many things for sale and quite cheap. So I asked housekeeper John to suggest to the cook a little variation from beancurd! But inevitably when we arrived at the table, there was the old thing again. Evidently Yin-chang and his wife liked it, it was easy to prepare, no peeling like potatoes or carrots, and they had long been accustomed to cook only what they pleased.

The last day of the week arrived, and we left early in the morning to work the far end of the plain, so we knew we might not be back until dark.

"I'll be very hungry by supper-time, John. Please make sure that Yin-chang buys some potatoes and carrots! Something I can eat," I pleaded.

"All right, dear," said John and I heard him give the order. So I set out complacent that by night time I would have a square meal. It was a beautiful morning: the golden air had a cheery nip of winter in it, and the little lake at the far end sparkled its blue waters into the yellow sunshine. In the centre of the plain spread the rice fields, and at the rim little hamlets were marked out by feathery green clusters of bamboo growing beside adobe houses.

From farm to farm we went. I played the guitar to draw a crowd, we all sang in Chinese, and when a group had gathered John and Mr. Yang preached. I talked with the women and children and we gave out tracts before moving on to the next clay-walled farmyard. Everyone was friendly, but when noon came no one offered us anything to eat. I began to feel very hungry for I had not been able to eat a big breakfast when it was just rice and beancurd.

"Oh, just endure a bit, dear," said John. "This is missionary life. It takes time to walk as far as this, and I want to visit every farm at this end of the plain before we go back. Perhaps we can buy some food at the next place."

But we never could. So it continued all day long. John was four years younger than I and at the beginning of our married life he had a tendency to drive me beyond my strength, not realizing that I really did not have the physical reserve he had.

Once we were able to buy some Chinese toffee, but my empty stomach resented sweets. By the time we had returned to the inn I was faint as well as weary. I kept struggling on, thinking of meat and potatoes, with perhaps some carrots.

Up the stairs of the inn we went and I was able to sit on my bed while John brought me a basin of water to wash off the dust.

"Is supper ready, Yin-chang?"

"Yes, Pastor. We will bring it right up."

It felt good to wash the dirt off, and Ying-chang and wife were arranging bowls of a steaming something in the middle of the table. I came over and looked. Beancurd. Even the meat had not been cooked separately but mixed in with the gray flannel squares!

"Where are the potatoes and carrots?" I asked.

Yin-chang looked at his wife and she looked at him. Obviously neither had paid any attention to that order.

"We didn't see any on the market today," they answered unitedly.

"Is there *nothing* else to eat?" I asked, desperately disappointed.

"Nothing."

It was too much for me. I fell on my face on the bed and wept. John urged me to self-control but I was too tired. I cried and cried, and finally cried myself to sleep.

Before midnight I woke up, my stomach gnawing with emptiness until it hurt. I sat up and hubby came over to me and said anxiously, "Won't you try to eat a little rice, at least, dear! I'll get Yin-chang to heat some up for you."

"All right, I'll try a little," I said weakly. A few minutes later John handed me a bowl of warm rice *with beancurd on the top*! But do you know, it did not taste so scorched-flannely this time. In fact, one bowl downed, I held it out for a second helping! And from then on, in my missionary life, beancurd and I were friends. I never grew very fond of it, but it was no longer obnoxious. As it was very nutritious I often had it on our own table at home, with a dish of some more tempting vegetable alongside.

This episode became a family joke. From then on, whenever some new Chinese dish appeared which did not appeal to me, my husband would be sure to say, "Maybe if you cried a little first you would enjoy it, Belle!"

The day was to come when I would learn to meet life's disappointments dry-eyed. There would even be an hour when my husband himself would say wistfully that a few tears were sometimes a good thing. But it takes time to grow. And it takes more than one season *to mellow.*

CHAPTER FIVE

HIS WONDERFUL COOK—AS VIEWED BY HER

YIN-CHANG'S laziness, however, continued to be a sore point.

I had started out meaning to be a very kind mistress. Chinese never gave their servants time off, but I arranged that Yin-chang and wife have a half day a week, and in every other way I watched for their comfort—until I found it was quite unnecessary! Their comfort was their own prime concern.

Once on a piercingly cold day, sitting motionless studying with the Chinese teacher, we both became so chilled that I ordered a brazier of burning charcoal. Yin-chang was a long time bringing it, and finally appeared with a tiny thing which I had never seen before, and in it a few black coals just beginning to ignite. It gave out almost no heat so the teacher and I continued to shiver. Knowing we had a good-sized new brazier I grew suspicious, excused myself and went in search of our helpers. It was early morning and there were no servants in sight at all. So I made for their bedroom. Sure enough! There, doing nothing, sat the two of them around our big brazier piled high with red-hot coals, toasting their toes in luxurious ease. The origin of the tiny pot was obvious—they had given us theirs and spared only a coal or two to start it. No, there was no need for me to be anxiously solicitous for their welfare!

In fact their demands increased. In that area country Chinese never took baths in bathtubs—they did not possess such things— but these two had decided that they must have everything which John and Isobel Kuhn had. So I found Yin-chang one day carrying my zinc tub to their bedroom.

"What are you doing with that, Yin-chang?" I asked.

"My wife wishes to take a bath," he answered blandly. But his wife had the itch—I was treating her for it!

"Let her use the tub downstairs, then," I said, "She has the itch and it is catching. I do not wish you to use ours." He made a sour face but had to comply.

A day or so later, after she had been into our bedroom, she came out smelling strongly of my perfume, one only bottle which I had brought from home to help me over moments when certain odours were a little too much for me, and that particular brand of perfume was not sold in our part of China! The inference was obvious, but she most indignantly denied it, saying it was her own perfume. I asked to see her bottle; as a bride she had some but it was packed away carefully in her suitcase and the scent was very different. When I pointed this out, she went to bed for two days and sulked, refusing to do any work whatever. Yin-chang declared she was ill.

Climaxes are not geysers that suddenly appear. They are mountains of small incidents, gradually piling up until they reach a peak.

This time the topping experience was so trivial, that I do not remember the matter at all. Yin-chang had failed in some duty, and when I pointed it out to John in the boy's presence (hoping to get it corrected) John turned on me, siding with Yin-chang.

Hot with temper, I said nothing, but put on my hat and coat and walked out of the house. Down through the town and out on to the plain, angry resentment boiling within. I was not going to live in a house where a lazy servant was condoned and preferred to the mistress! And so on. For hours I walked, blind as to direction, not caring what happened to me—but just determined to get away from it all.

Finally I was brought to myself by the curious glances of the Chinese. Little villages studded that plain, and I must have been in one of them when dusk fell. A woman alone on the road as dark was falling! It was not done. Good women were in their homes at such an hour. And for the first time, the tumult of my own feelings fell into enough quiet for that still small Voice to be heard.

"You have not considered Me and My honour, in all this, have you?" said the Voice. "You came to this land to make Me known. How much of Me has anyone learned from you this day, do you think?" I was appalled.

"Oh dear Lord, I'm sorry. It is true. I've been full of myself and my hurt feelings. What can I do?"

"You can go back," said the Voice relentlessly. I thought again of Yin-chang's smirking face and groaned and flinched.

"But, oh Lord, how can I endure the humiliation? The servants are laughing at me."

"How do you think I endure the humiliation you have brought on Me before these people?" said the Voice. "You have not invited Me into this servant situation. You've just tried to manage by your own wits." Then and there I invited Him, humbly pleaded with Him to work it out for me and—turned my steps homeward.

What happens when the Irresistible Force collides with the Immovable Object? The first reaction was to bounce off on a path of its own.

Back in the little wooden upstairs the Immovable Object sat still at his desk. Outwardly he was studying Chinese but inwardly a gloomy feeling that something had gone wrong with the universe was depressing him. This wife of his—if she was angry, why had she not said so? In his good Pennsylvania Dutchland people spoke their minds out, talked it back and forth, you know, then a fellow could explain his side. But to flash you an angry look and then just walk out! He squirmed uncomfortably in his seat.

Where had she gone anyway? An hour or more had passed. Why did she not come back? What if she did not come back? The thought made him go hot all over. Mighty embarrassing to have to explain to people. If there was anything that he hated it was a thing like this. But maybe he had been a little at fault too. If he had only waited until Yin-chang had left before he rebuked her. That was probably what had vexed her—to side with the servant in that servant's presence. Of course he had not actually excused Yin-chang; it all happened so suddenly. And why did she always have to be noticing the things that were wrong with Yin-chang! Got along with him perfectly well before marriage—why not after? Of course he had never checked Yin-chang closely, and Yin-chang's wife did not seem to be very helpful, that was sure. Well, it was getting dark. What if she did not!—but at that moment she did! Conquered by the *really Irresistible*

Force, in the door walked the *so-called* Irresistible Force, a humbled and grief-stricken wife.

"Oh! You're back!" What a relief! Looking at her curiously he asked, "Where did you go?"

"Out the west gate." An unusual quietness was still upon her.

"Well, it is past supper time. I've already eaten, but I'll call Yin-chang to heat up yours."

Little was said either during the meal, or for the rest of the evening over Chinese study books. But each felt a gentleness in the other that had not been there before.

After their Bible reading together and prayer together before retiring, the Immovable Object suddenly said, "You may dismiss Yin-chang and his wife, if they bother you that much. But I do not know whom you can get in their place to help you—servants are hard to find."

Wonder of wonders, how did such a renunciation come about! The *really* Irresistible Force had been at work in this heart also. What a difference when we invite Him into the situation!

"Thank you, dear. I know it costs you to say that. I know it would mean a lot to you to turn Yin-chang out; but really, if he is going to cause trouble between us—nothing is worth that much is it? I don't mind doing the work myself. We will just have to ask the Lord to find us another helper. Anything is better than what I've been through today."

And then the bridegroom got a tender kiss in token of love's sacrifice.

It is only fair to point out that Yin-chang had not been so difficult to deal with before his marriage. When John and he were both bachelors, they did much travelling and preaching together. John encouraged him to take his turn at public witness for Christ. Thus they often stood shoulder to shoulder in open-air meetings, or sat side by side in tea-shops, talking of Christ to others. This inevitably led to regard and mutual affection.

As we watched later events, it was obvious that Yin-chang got the wrong wife. She was a nominal Christian, but had joined the church only to please her family. Following the Chinese custom of engaged couples rarely seeing each other, he did not know her well, but her pretty face satisfied him, and did not reveal the proud, lazy and selfish nature behind it. Once married, all her counsel was for self-advancement; and it was not hard to push Yin-chang into taking advantage of his intimacy with John. To dismiss his old comrade of the preaching trail was truly hard.

The next morning I told Yin-chang and his wife that their service was not satisfactory, and that they might go home. Of course Yin-chang went immediately to John, expecting the triumph of the day before, but did not receive it.

Yin-chang and his wife went off to their bedroom and closed the door. They did no work, but neither did they make the slightest move to leave! I could hardly wait to see the last of them, clean up the place, and get it into the order which my soul longed for. But I had yet to learn that dismissing a servant in the Orient was not the simple matter it is at home.

The following morning I had my first experience of trying to light an open grate fire and cook breakfast on it. As I was struggling with the smoke and coals that would not ignite, John came up to me, took the fan, and said gravely, "I'll fan this. You are wanted downstairs." Wondering who could want me at that early hour, and quite forgetting the regular morning Bible class, I descended the wooden stairs to the chapel beneath our two rooms. To my consternation, there was the whole church board of deacons seated looking at me, with Yin-chang, triumphant, in the background.

"Please be seated, Mrs. Kuhn," said the town postmaster, who was also the leading elder. He was very solemn and immediately began a long grave dissertation. My heart beat with panic—it has always been easier for me to speak a foreign language than to understand it—and being nervous I was soon lost in his flow of speech.

"Excuse me a moment," I said, "I do not understand. May I go for Pastor Kuhn to interpret for me, please!" and turning I flew up the stairs.

"John!" I gasped, "you've got to come and help me! Do come down and interpret for me! How can I answer when I do not understand what they've said?"

"Well," said my spouse slowly, "guess I can do that much."

So down the two of us went, and the solemn diaconate proceeded to review this rather serious affair. The sum of the postmaster's remarks was this: they, the church deacons, had helped Pastor Kuhn secure these two Christian servants. And they understood that Pastor Kuhn himself had been quite satisfied with Yin-chang's services in the past. Was that so, Pastor Kuhn?

Face grave, Pastor Kuhn bowed his head in affirmation.

But now Mrs. Kuhn says they must be dismissed. Would she kindly explain why? Had they stolen anything? A profound silence, every ear turned to hear the answer. No, they had not been dishonest.

Had there been any immoral conduct? No. What then was their crime? And eight pairs of disapproving black eyes were fastened upon me. I felt like a culprit at the bar, and Yin-chang was grinning broadly now.

Humiliated and trembling with excitement, I tried to explain their laziness and impudence. I related the story of their using our big brazier and giving us their tiny one. But the Chinese mouths merely curled in derision. Of course servants were lazy, else they would not be in that class but would have the enterprise to set up business for themselves. What else did you expect?

Just when my hope had ebbed, and life seemed to have lost all its savour, the postmaster turned and addressed Yin-chang. "You had better pack up your belongings then, and go home." The relief which that word brought me gave strength to see the meeting to an end. That day Yin-chang and his wife packed their things and left us.

And now I was to find out that Yin-chang had been of some use after all. My early morning prayer time was broken into by having to light that fire on the primitive Chinese cooking stove. I had to learn from experience that when I did not balance the pots carefully and one tipped its water a little, a cloud of ashes would rise in the air and descend all over me, the stove and the meal. And if enough water happened to spill, it would put out the fire! Breakfast finally accomplished, I must go to the market and buy the meat and vegetables for the day. There were no fixed prices in those days and every single thing had to be bargained for. This gave some language practice but took far too much time. I might return home to find there had been women visitors, but after long waiting for me they had left.

John, of course, pitched in and helped me with the lighting

of fires and marketing. For that first morning he felt it would be good if I learned the seriousness of dismissing servants whom the church had provided for us. And it was a lesson which I needed.

But there was washing and ironing which proved time-consuming. To haul up every drop of water in a bucket from the well, try to get some heated, then sit and rub clothes by hand—hours went by. And the ironing, with flat-irons heated on open charcoal—as often as I wiped them off it seemed that a speck of soot would dance down on the shirt before me and get ironed into a black streak before I knew it had landed! I wondered how Mrs. Yin-chang had ever turned out such clean clothes for us! And often in the midst of these busy days I would hear an echo of the deacon's voice, "There are worse things than laziness."

As days went by and I felt myself unduly tied to secondary things, we began to make the servant problem a matter of prayer. The Lord needed to be invited into this affair, and when He was, He took command as only He can. He sent to us a young married woman who had been deserted by her husband and left so destitute that the very clothes she had on her back were borrowed! She was a heathen and her family notoriously crooked.

To show me that there were able Chinese servants in this world, she proved to be the cleverest, most industrious helper I ever had until I went to Lisuland. I had to show her how to do things only once, and my burden in that regard was lifted permanently. Best of all, I was able to lead her to trust the Lord Jesus as her personal Saviour. Unfortunately for me, when we were soon called to move to the west, Mrs. Chang's husband, finding her well clothed and with money in her pocket, claimed her back, and I had to leave her with him. I put her in touch with the nearest missionary and never saw her again; but I trust I shall, in heaven.

CHAPTER SIX

SPEECH SEASONED WITH SALT

"BELLE, it's come! We are appointed to move west and take over the station of Tali which has been without missionaries for a year now. Whoopee!" John waved the letter from headquarters at me with jubilation. I ran to him, and we hugged each other with joyous exuberance, then stopped to join in a prayer of thanksgiving to God. *The Lisu tribes of J. O. Fraser's discovery were in western Yunnan.*

"There's another letter," went on John. "Mr. Fraser wishes us to come up to Kunming in May. He will be there at that time, and would like to see us before we go west. Also Jack Graham and Ella are being married on May 15, and Mr. Fraser knows they want us as best man and matron of honour. So it is all working out. Then too, Bud F—— is having to come to Kunming for new glasses. Belle, you will get to meet Bud at last!"

Bud had been John's special friend and confidant at Chinese Language School, 1926-28. During the term, one of their fellow-students, William Potts, had suddenly died. God had used his death to solemnize and challenge that group of new workers. Bud and John had rededicated themselves to God, and the Lord had used them to challenge others. John was especially blessed by the truth of *Christ living in the believer*. It had transformed his life.

Bud had been sent to a different province so he and I had never met. He was slim, good looking and had dimples. Not what I would conjure up for a male saint! But as soon as you started to talk to him you forgot everything but the Lord. He lived for no one else and nothing else. In his presence my Irish effervescence soon quieted down and a great wistfulness for God came to me.

That night John was asked to preach in the street chapel, but as I was weary I went to bed instead. The evening streets brought mostly men to the chapel anyway. But before I was asleep, John burst into our room.

"Belle! Say, Bud wants me to pray all night with him in the chapel. Do you mind, dear, when it is for this purpose?"

I answered slowly, "No-o, I don't mind. But I'd like to know why! Why wouldn't an hour of prayer be enough?"

"Well," said Hubby resignedly, "guess I'll have to tell you. They asked Bud and me to preach in street chapel, and as Bud went first, I couldn't help but compare his Chinese with mine. We came to China together, you know. He speaks the language O.K., but I couldn't help but know that my language was better. No one responded to the gospel invitation, and the meeting finally closed. As Bud approached me, I guess I rather expected to have him compliment me on the progress I'd made since last he heard me." Here Hubby stopped and hung his head.

I was very proud of his fluent Chinese, and added "Well?"

"Well, Bud said to me, 'John, I was disappointed tonight. You have made great progress with the language, of course, but when last I heard you speak I used to see the Christ. Tonight I could not get by John Kuhn and his fine command of the language. No one was won to Christ tonight, was there? Do you suppose you've lost something? Would you like to pray with me all night if need be—just you and I? Besides, I feel I need it. In the province where I was sent the churches are so cold. There has been argument between senior missionaries as to which Chinese term should be used for "God" in preaching and trans-lation. Oh, is Satan to kill our usefulness just by side-tracking us? I feel I need to pray, but I'd like to have you pray with me, as we used to do in Shanghai.' I told him that I wanted to ask you first, but I was sure you wouldn't hinder."

"I most surely won't," I replied, deeply stirred. "And tell him I'll be praying here too. It took courage to speak to you straight like that, when he was the poorer speaker of the two."

"Yes," acquiesced Hubby humbly, "but God comes first with Bud, you know. And I want that He should with us, too. I needed this correction badly."

"Bless you, dear," I said. "Go and the Lord be with you."

That all-night prayer meeting was the beginning of revival blessing among us all. The work in Yunnan was not dead as in Bud's province, but we had had differences between senior missionaries, too, and our superintendent felt we all needed a fresh touch from the Lord. So he called as many together as could come, and proclaimed a cessation of all but most necessary work that the rest of the time might be spent in prayer and meeting together.

The ten days that followed we never forgot. Truly the Lord met us. The Holy Spirit convicted first one, then another. With tears we confessed critical thoughts or wrong actions to one another, and there was a putting away of hindering things, with a real melting together. This was the first time in my life that behind-the-back criticism of another Christian was shown to me to be *sin*—and a most deadly sin that paralyses the Spirit, and quenches Him when He is longing to pour out blessing. I wish that I could say that I was never again guilty of this, but that would not be true. It did mean, however, that from that day I *recognized* it as wrong and something that I must treat as sin.

Our superintendent, Mr. J. O. Fraser, was wonderful in this regard. In his speech seasoned with salt he was an example to all of us. Besides, he was courageous enough to refuse to listen to criticism of another when it was made to him. Now we wonder, if Bud had been afraid to say to John what in his heart, he knew needed to be said, what would have been the end! We do not like to think.

After the conference you can imagine our anticipation as John and I started west for Tali, an old station but at the moment without missionaries. We were to continue Chinese language studies there, but also to help young missionaries whom the Mission was expecting. There had been an appeal for two hundred new workers in two years, and the first of these would soon arrive. Mr. Fraser thought it was extremely important with whom young missionaries spent their first years, and we were made to feel our responsibility. John was also to itinerate and explore the areas around Tali.

Those days there was no Burma Road. We had to travel stage by stage; either walking, or riding on a horse or in a *hwa-gan* (mountain chair). At night we stopped at whatever little town we had come to. It was slow, weary travel, but the beauty of Yunnan mountains far repaid the weariness; and the opportunity to present the gospel at night in the little stopping places was worth the time consumed. I much prefer it to the dangerous ride in Burma Road trucks of later years, where you finished a week's travel in two days and lost all those little town contacts.

It was during our third stage out from Kunming that I contracted dysentery (the same kind as in Acts 28:8), and was dangerously ill. So we had to stop off at Tsuhsiung. An American missionary lived there in a beautiful big compound and she also had a little Christian Chinese nurse, Miss Ling, staying with her. For three weeks Miss Ling nursed me. She had nursed many such cases in Shanghai, but said she had never seen one so bad as mine. Yet the Lord brought me through.

It was on June 28, 1930, that we arrived at Tali. John had wanted me to walk with him from Hsia-kuan. Our coolies had stopped there for the night, although it was still early afternoon. The Chinese had told us that Tali was just "san-*si* li" (three or four Chinese miles) farther on; in fact they meant "san-*shih* li," but pronounced it differently. We thought three or four li (Chinese miles) was meant, when it actually was thirty li!

The road was level all the way and very beautiful scenery absorbed our attention. To the left, the high range of mountains which contain the Azure Peak, 15,000 feet altitude; to the right, emerald green rice fields sloping away to a large blue lake. Tali is the marble quarry of China, and the villages through which we passed were all built of stone—quaint, picturesque dwellings. Every now and then we crossed a rushing crystal mountain stream of melted snow.

I was still weak from sickness, and it was the end of the day to boot, so I soon tired. But John urged me on, eager to see our new station. I went as long as I could, but when I said, "John, I can't go any farther," I meant just that.

"Oh, you're doing fine, dear, just a few more steps. See, here is the gate," he reassured me.

But I could not make those steps. He half carried me in and laid me on the floor—the only place available, for the house was empty.

"Belle, you're awful!" he said, standing over me perplexed. "When you say you're through, you just stop. You don't make any further effort."

"But, dear," I argued weakly, "I don't say I'm through until I am!"

Help was on its way. The Chinese Pastor lived in the front part of the extensive compound which was the C.I.M. Home in Tali. He soon came in to see us, and inquired if we had made arrangements for supper. After a long rest and some warm food, I was able to sit up, and even walk a little. John had already been all over the place. Such a domain after our two small windowless rooms in Chengchiang!

I still remember the thrill of the first evening when he led me through the rooms of the "Cloisters of Tali", as later they were named. Three wings of rooms, upper and lower, were absolutely ours, a lawn, and a huge garden at the back, not to speak of the small court between the wings, which was planted with flowering trees. It was luxury and paradise to us. Gentle, refined young Pastor Li was always so concerned for our comfort—we just loved him from the first contact on. It was at Tali that we preached and ministered for two and a half years, and there our first child was born.

CHAPTER SEVEN

WHEN WE BECAME PARENTS

JOHN was only twenty-three years old when we were married, and he was not much interested in babies. He wanted to be able to take me round with him when he itinerated.

At the end of our first year, I knew that God was going to give us a child, and I broke the news with a bit of inner perturbation—would John be vexed? But I had many surprises coming to me from this same "Daddy." He was delighted! A radiant light beamed on his face, and he cried out: "Great news! I hope it's a boy. Then when the Chinese ask me: 'Yang Muh-szu, yu-mu-yu er-tzu, ma?' I'll be able to answer, 'Yu ih-ko; yu ih-ko hsiao tu-shu-ti.'" (Pastor Kuhn, have you any children? Yes, one—a small schoolboy.)

But I did not want John to get his heart set on a boy, lest it turn out to be a girl! So I flashed back: "Yes, but what if you have to answer: 'It's a small cook-rice-to-eat one'?" (Hsiao chu-fan-ch'ih-tih.)

"Oh, that will be all right too," answered the thrilled and happy Daddy-in-prospect. "But where is the baby to be born? The nearest hospital is Kunming. Are you going all that long way back? It will be only a year since we left there! I don't like to go trotting back to the capital city so soon. It would take a big scoop out of our time."

"That's what I think, too," I replied. "I've been thinking of Miss Ling, at Tsuhsiung. She nursed me through dysentery, remember? I happen to know that she is a midwife with lots of experience, trained by Dr. Mary Stone of Bethel Mission in Shanghai. She'd be capable, I'm sure!"

"The very one!"

So it was arranged. John, who had now become skilled in Chinese writing, carried on the correspondence with Miss Ling.

John and I had no idea we were doing anything hazardous. That a woman expecting her first baby needs more medical

check-ups than others had never occurred to us. Mails were overland and slow. There was no air mail to those parts. So it was a
long, long time before we learned how anxious some of the older
women in the Mission were that I had not seen a doctor, did not
plan to see one, and was trusting everything to a Chinese nurse!
By that time it was too late to get me out to a hospital, so they
did what remained to do. *They prayed hard for us!* And I came
through wonderfully.

It was March, 1931 when Miss Ling arrived. And already we
had junior workers. Ernest Mansfield and Will Allen had been
studying Chinese under John's tutoring for some months by
that time. They were two young bachelors, full of devotion to
the Lord, but also blessed with a sense of humour which helped
us fit in to one another. (Ernest was Australian, Will was English,
born in China, and educated at our C.I.M. School at Chefoo.)

Miss Ling was a slight, small young woman with a business-
like manner. She had a book on obstetrics with her, and showed
me the gruesome pictures in it of unnatural presentations and
instrument cases. I wished she had not—they haunted me! Now
I knew what was possible, and I shuddered. But she was very
casual.

"Oh, don't worry. I've delivered each of these special cases,
and all by myself too! It is experience that counts. Now you will
probably have long labour at your age (29). Walk! Get out and
exercise those muscles, limber them up."

Sensitive to grinning Chinese with knowing looks, I hunted
for a walk where I resorted every morning, walking back and
forth, praying or studying Chinese for several hours at a time.
Much did I pray for the little "boy-student" or "girl-cook" who
was coming to us. I had been reading a book in which the author
said: "But Elspeth was God's child alway."[1] I liked that. So I
asked it for our first born, "May he or she be God's child
always!"

When the time came Miss Ling had everything prepared in
our own big, airy bedroom on the second floor. She was very
efficient, but as the first pains made me catch my breath and
wince, she said, "Oh, that's nothing! They'll get much worse
than that!"

[1] *Sentimental Tommy*, by James Barrie.

It was my dear husband who was my pillar of strength at the trying hour.

At 11.40 p.m., April 10, 1931, a thin wail pierced the lamp-lit room and Kathryn Ann Kuhn had made her appearance in this old world.

As soon as baby was taken away by nurse to be bathed, John knelt and, taking my hand, thanked our dear Lord for the merciful delivery, and for our little daughter. "And Lord," he prayed, "we give her back to Thee. We lay no claim to her. We want her to be Thine and serve Thee all her life."

I was awakened the next morning by a call from baby's alcove. Her window opened close to Ernest Mansfield's. It was John's voice. He had been waiting to see if Ernest was awake, and as soon as he discerned movement, he called out "Ernest!"

From my bed I could see Ernest's face come to the window. Then John held up his arms with something cradled in them. "It's born!" he answered in ecstasy, "It's a girl! I'll bring it over for you to see."

"Oh, don't bother, she might catch cold," called back Ernest. "I'll come over to your place. I'll call Will too."

I was smiling at my husband's boyishness. No new toy had ever caught his boyhood's fancy and swung him off his feet like that little girlie. I could see her face was still red and wrinkled, and wondered how the two bachelors were going to salve their consciences and yet please their senior missionary!

Ernest, always kind and sympathetic, had done some successful thinking on his way up the stairs. "Oh, isn't she a dear!" he exclaimed enthusiastically. That did it. Daddy beamed. Enthusiasm was all he needed; the reasons for it were not important. Then John turned expectantly to Will.

"They say she looks like me," he suggested hopefully. Will's honesty was knocked off balance. He gave a quick laugh. "Oh come now, John, you really . . ." But sympathetic Ernest had been bending over baby. He straightened up and said, "Yes, I think she does, John. The shape of her head is yours, round with a square jaw. Isobel's head is long and thin, and the jaw almost pointed. Yes, that jaw declares her a Kuhn!"

"You really think so, do you?" complacently murmured

Daddy. He was sublimely happy and the bachelors' visit had been a great success.

Kathy's redness faded soon, of course, and the wrinkles smoothed out, with little cheeks of apple-blossom velvet. She had had from the first beautiful black curly eyelashes, and when the time came that she began to laugh, her hazel eyes sparkled like topaz. Charm is a thing difficult to describe, but Mummy somehow thought that she was going to have that when she grew up.

It is not Oriental custom to show a baby to visitors during the first month. In fact, among the Chinese peasants of our parts and among the Lisu too, even the mother was not available to friends for the first four weeks. But Daddy burst all such bounds. Our wonderful baby was the first topic of conversation, and sleeping or no, she must be produced for every visitor.

While we were discussing a Chinese name for our baby one morning, someone was playing the gramophone: "Grace that is greater than all our sins." As the chorus floated up to us, "Grace, grace, God's grace . . ." both of us, almost simultaneously, exclaimed: "There it is, let's call her Hong-En (Vast-Grace) in memory of God's goodness to us."

She was dedicated to God in the chapel at Tali at the end of the thirty days. It happened that the country pastor, Mr. Li, had a baby girl named Heo-En (Great-Grace) also one month old. So the Chinese and American babies were dedicated at the same time, we parents also standing up together. And of course we gave a feast to the Chinese to celebrate our little girl's one-month birthday.

Twelve years passed before Daddy had a repetition of the joy of fatherhood. It is true we once hoped to have a second child who would be a playmate for Kathy. But due to over exertion during a time of stormy flood and fright, I lost that hope.

We were then in the wild canyon of the Upper Salween, and the Japanese War was in full spate. Indeed the Japanese were just across the river from us. To go out to the hospital would mean not being able to return until the war was over. One had to get a military pass from the Chinese Government to come into the mountain where we lived (considered front line of battle for a short time). They would never give such permission to a woman and baby. If I went out I must stay out. But I had just been definitely led *into* the canyon.

Then God worked. Miss Dorothy Burrows, one of our English nurses at Tali hospital, was due a vacation. She loved the tribes work and volunteered to come, taking that in lieu of her vacation. There was a Chinese guerrilla Colonel who had offered to get her a military pass and escort her in! Truly it seemed of the Lord.

But once again, with a confinement that was not ordinary (I was nearly 42 years old and conditions arose which took expert skill), I did not once see a doctor, but was very efficiently cared for by an experienced nurse. The baby chose to appear on Sunday, August 1, 1943, just as the Lisu were leaving church. We were living at Maliping (Oak Flat Village) and many from surrounding villages came there for the noonday service.

We had been hoping for a son, so Nurse Burrows was jubilant as she brought the little bundle to me, saying "It is Daniel, all right!"

"Now I can answer the Chinese, 'One of each' when they ask if I have children!" said Daddy. And that was the first inkling he had given Mummy that he had felt the stigma of not having a son. For twelve years he had been politely asked about his children, and had had to answer, "Only one, a daughter."

To see big Daddy walking round with the little golden head resting in the crook of his arm, was a thrill I never forgot. Daddy wanted to take his son everywhere; to watch the volley ball game at play-hour, to go for a walk over the mountainside, and when they came back there was a wild flower set into the tiny fist "for Mummy."

His name was chosen for love of the young Jewish prophet who "purposed in his heart not to defile himself." For the Chinese and Lisu to pronounce "Daniel" was simple. Their Bibles transliterated it *Da-nay-lee*.

CHAPTER EIGHT

THE UNWANTED ASSIGNMENT

TWO happy years were spent in that big beautiful home in Tali.

It was in 1931, some months before Kathryn was born that our nearest missionaries, ten days' journey west at Paoshan, gave us an invitation to come over and help them in a special evangelistic effort at their station. The call *Westward Ho* has always stirred our blood, so we accepted joyfully. (And incidentally the senior missionary at Paoshan could take charge of my fourth oral Chinese language exam.)

On such trips John usually rode a horse or walked and I rode a mountain chair.

One particular afternoon we were winding up and over mountain tops for a long time. I was wondering where we would sleep that night—the sun had begun to lower, yet we were still wandering over wild uninhabited mountains. Suddenly John, walking a little distance ahead of me, disappeared! I got out of the mountain chair and began to walk, hoping thus to speed up my slow carriers. I hallooed John but there was no answer. He had turned to wave to me just before going around the crest of a peak, so I hurried up that little slope, turned the corner and—gasped. The mountain fell away from my feet in a steep drop to tiers of lower hills of graduating heights, like colossal steps descending. There, far below was John, a mere speck on the path that circled one of the tiers before it dropped to the next hill. He turned to look for me, saw me, and waved!

The range had fallen away into a beautiful little green valley, at least two thousand feet beneath us, and through the valley ran a stream shining like a silver ribbon through emerald fields with a sunset glory gilding the opposite mountain bank. From the other side of the valley rose tier after tier of hills until it levelled off even with where I now stood, making me feel as if I were on top of the world. It was the valley of Yungping (meaning Eternal Peace). And we were to spend the night in the little market town huddled against the foot of the western hills. Far below me John was signalling with his arms that I should hurry up. Reluctant to leave that most wonderful panorama, I knew by the setting sun that I must.

The population was mostly Muslim. That night, after our supper, we went out on the street for an open-air meeting, as was our custom. But the audience was unmoved, stony-faced and indifferent. John felt depressed. As we prepared for bed in the dusty little inn, he said to me, "I suppose someone will be asked to come here and open this plain to the gospel. A missionary has never lived here, so there has never been a thorough presentation of the message. I pity the person that has to tackle this job. Maybe Mr. Fraser will ask Will to come here." (Will Allen was noted among us as always rising to the occasion!)

Neither John nor I dreamed that *we* would be the ones Mr. Fraser would assign to this difficult task. Yet it was so.

Mr. Fraser had never intended that missionaries should stay on in an old established work like Tali. The Chinese Christians should run their own church eventually, while there were still many large areas of West Yunnan unevangelized. Therefore, when the last batch of Forward Movement workers had been sent to us, Mr. Fraser suggested that we ourselves open up a new district, and Eternal-Peace was the place he named.

I have seldom seen my husband more downcast. The work at Tali he had loved. For him it had been a joy to explore the needy fields around Tali, to help in the initial preaching efforts. But now to be confined to one valley of such indifferent and difficult people as Muslims! To me the appointment was quite agreeable. I had fallen in love with the beautiful little plain. I was also glad to get back to life nearer the nationals. Tali was on the main road of travel, and for me as hostess there was much entertaining of missionaries of other missions, not to mention world-explorers and hunters. I had lost several of my Chinese Bible classes through the constant interruption of unexpected Western visitors.

I was happy at the prospect of an area big enough for a life-work, but small enough that I would always get back home by nightfall and sleep in my own clean bed! I did not like travel. But I felt sorry for John.

The work in the church and country around Tali had been thriving, but now blessing seemed to leave and sickness struck us. We had recently received four young men as new workers, when I came down with a fever we could not diagnose. There was no doctor nearer than Kunming, at that time a two weeks journey away. Nurse Ruth Colquhoun (later Mansfield) was summoned from Mitu. She came gladly, but she had never seen a fever like it. Searching the medical books she felt that black-water fever was the nearest in description to what I was experiencing.

I grew steadily weaker and John became concerned for my life. As he knelt at my bed praying that I might be allowed to recover, the Lord spoke to him about his own inner unwillingness for our new assignment. There was a keen struggle. Then he yielded. I began to improve. But I was exceedingly weak when the fever left me, and almost had to learn to walk anew.

St. Francis de Sales said, "If He calls you to a kind of service which is according to His will but not according to your taste, you must not go to it with less, rather with more courage and energy, than if your taste coincided with His will."

Blessing began to flow again. So we found a definite relationship between inner surrender and outward blessing, which is another proof of a living God.

In those two and a half years at Tali (1930-32) we received ten new workers, helped them get through their first language exams, rented premises and assisted them to get started in six different towns, including Yungping. Each place had a whole plain full of Chinese until then unevangelized. Besides, in and around Tali, souls were saved, John and I finished the required language examinations, and Kathryn was born to us.

CHAPTER NINE

BEGINNINGS AT YUNGPING

AT the northern end of the plain of Yungping was a little town called Old Market. The population here was not so wholly Muslim, and John was blessed in obtaining an old native house on the river bank. There were three wings around a little courtyard, the fourth side of which was the river walk. Everywhere lay the unwashed dirt of years and black sooty walls. John was disheartened at the task of cleaning it up and repairing it, but I saw possibilities in its spaciousness, and loved the privacy of the river bank.

"Don't worry," I assured him gaily, "Sally and I will soon clean it up and transform it!"

Sally Kelly, who later became Mrs. Stuart Harverson, was our newest young worker, and she was to live with us during her first language study days. She was a Scottish girl from my own home town of Vancouver. Unselfish, capable and devoted, she also sparkled with wit and humour. The longer we knew her the more we loved her.

God prospered us, too, in getting the help of two fine Chinese carpenters, a father and son, who not only repaired the house, putting in wooden floors and windows, but also made furniture for us. They charged a lump sum for two months' labour and as they were very industrious it made the cost of repairs and furniture quite reasonable.

There had been the matter of servants. John was for waiting until we got to Yungping, and then hiring some local residents and training them. But Kathryn was about a year and a half old when we moved to Yungping—just the toddling age when she must be watched carefully, especially as we lived so near the river.

I had been warned by one who was born a child of the C.I.M. never to leave my children to national amahs, or let the heathen play with them promiscuously. Evil habits and speech can be learned in early childhood that are difficult to eradicate later. So I was always very careful and watchful with my little one. Our cook, Mrs. Hwang, was a widow with only one child, a daughter about thirteen years old, named Small Pearl. Small Pearl was a spoiled child, but she was a pure little thing and took care of our small Kathryn. So I wished to bring mother and daughter with us to Yungping.

"You know that Mrs. Hwang is not satisfactory," argued John.

"Yes," I replied, "but who is to market and cook and watch Kathryn while we clean that sooty house? I will be in no situation to train raw hands during the first week or so."

"All right, have it your own way," said my hubby good-naturedly, "But I'm afraid you'll be sorry." And oh, wasn't I!

Mrs. Hwang worked well at first and certainly did relieve me during the cleaning period. And Small Pearl was always reliable in caring for little Kathryn.

Downstairs in the central wing was to be the Chinese guest hall and dining-room, with a small room at the side for John's study. The long black hole upstairs was to be our bedroom. The carpenter put in a window or so, and then we set out to clean the room. It had been the ancestral worship hall, and placed against the wall was a long buffet-like table where idols had stood. There was no ceiling, but long soot-incrusted cobwebs hung from the roof tiles.

With hair tied up in a kerchief and broom in hand, Sally mounted this table to sweep the roof. She struck a dramatic attitude, and with outflung arm began, "Behold I . . . " Then *crash*! The house shook, black soot rained down upon us and I thought, for a second, that the end of the earth had come. I had instinctively shut my eyes in self-defence, but when I opened them in horror I saw a heap of soot-blackened rags on the floor before me, out from the top of which stared two startled sky-blue eyes. Those eyes were the only part of Sally Kelly still recognizable. The rest looked like the dirtiest chimney-sweep which Scotland ever produced. The table had had a broken leg and Sally's hundred pounds caused it to collapse. But the weight of the fall so shook the house that it acted as a roof cleaner. The soot of many years was knocked off and descended upon us. When we realized that no bones had been broken and saw that our roof was so unexpectedly cleaned for us, we laughed till we shook again. And this was typical of those days of repairing the breaches in Eternal Peace.

Soap and water and whitewash effected quite a transformation. Of course visitors were not lacking, and one of us was always free to witness to them.

We expected it would prove a hard place, so you can imagine our feelings when one afternoon a great racket outside our gate startled us and brought us all running.

Through our front gate a procession was marching. First came boys setting off firecrackers, "pop! pop! bang! bang!" "What's going on?" muttered John, going forward to receive them. For behind the fireworks was a single file of the leading citizens of Old Market, each carrying a tray with gifts on it! There was a handsome pair of scarlet satin scrolls on one: packages of sugar or tea on others, and so on.

Mystified but gracious, John showed them into the guest room and relieved them of the trays. The leading townsmen had come to welcome us to Eternal Peace, and they all meant to join us! They had heard about the Christian church and they noticed that Pastor Kuhn did not drink or smoke. Fine morality —they were all for it too, but gradually, of course. Buddhism was old-fashioned, they realized, and it would be wise to have something more modern. Just like a benefit society, you know. And they all beamed at John.

It was difficult, but also an excellent opportunity. John explained that Christianity was not a new kind of club, but a personal relationship to God based on His forgiveness of our sins. All men are sinners.

"Yes, yes," they nodded in grave assent, thinking that this was Pastor Kuhn's way of referring to wine and tobacco.

But when he got to "Thou shalt have no other gods before me," they began to talk. Perhaps *idols* were old-fashioned—they could go. But, of course, Pastor Kuhn would not ask them to give up *ancestor worship*. Why, that was the basic thing in Chinese culture! Confucius and Christ could get along quite well together, could they not? They were politely incredulous when told that Christians may worship no one but God—most decidedly not ancestors, who were but creatures of His creation.

"We may venerate our ancestors but not worship them," John said. In embarrassment they took their leave.

After John had politely escorted them to the door and warmly urged them to come again for more discussion, he returned to us.

"Did you ever see a more vivid illustration of what I've been reading these days? Campbell Morgan was saying in *The Acts of the Apostles*, 'Satan's first choice is to co-operate with us. Persecution is only his second-best method.' "

From then on, the work at Eternal Peace was just as difficult as we had preconceived it. Several illiterate peasant women were won to the Lord and a young fellow named Ma Fu-yin, who could read. His death before he was thirty left the little group of Christians without a leader. It was not until Communism took over years later, and with all the white missionaries gone, that an educated Chinese lady was led of the Lord to go to Eternal Peace. There she gleaned a harvest from seed long-sown and watered with prayers, and we heard that a little church was thriving in Eternal Peace, led by this Christian Chinese lady. But that is moving ahead of our story.

At first our cook was quite helpful, but as new young workers came to live with us (John helped them with the language and I relieved them of all housekeeping responsibilities so they had full time for language study), Mrs. Hwang relapsed into her old laziness. She would not buy or prepare enough food; she would not make bread when told to, but ran it so short that frequently we had to go a meal or so without any because her new batch had not risen, and so on. It caused me almost as much trouble as if I had to do it all myself. More and more she became a thorn in the flesh. But when I spoke of dismissing her, she immediately made preposterous claims. I must pay her for travel by sedan chair back to Tali and pay for an escort, as she was afraid to go alone. Then I would have to pay for a sedan chair for Small Pearl too, and coolies to carry their things. I had brought her so far from home I was responsible for her getting back. She made conditions that were impossible for us to fulfil, so we had to keep her on. Yet she grew worse and worse and quarrelled with everyone. I had to re-do her work daily until I was groaning with the bondage of it.

Then I began to commit this situation to the Lord. "Father, I confess I was wrong not to take John's advice at the beginning. He said I would rue it and I do. But is there no help for me now? I can't get rid of her but You could. Please take her from me." He did not choose to answer immediately. I was praying daily to be relieved of her for some three months before the freedom actually came.

Meanwhile Mrs. Hwang began to quarrel with everyone around her. She grew more and more cantankerous until the neighbours became angry at her and the women on the market turned against her. Of course she never admitted she was wrong, it was always everybody else who was mean! But with everyone everywhere disliking her she became so unhappy that she quit one day, of her own accord! She had met some horsemen from Tali who were going back and she hired a horse for herself. To me it was like a miracle.

Little Pearl was in tears. She had found her mother difficult to live with too, and she wanted to stay with us. We offered to keep her as Kathryn's nursemaid, and her mother, uncertain of her own future and expenses, gave consent. So the morning came when her mother departed.

The whole household decided to celebrate and have a spring cleaning. Mrs. Hwang had been supposed to do the sweeping and dusting, but as with everything else, it had been done very negligently. Now we all set to and cleaned the house thoroughly. John insisted we have our pictures taken—heads tied up in bandanas, brooms, dustpans and scrubbing pails well to the fore. Oh the fun of those days when we were all young!

The years proved Small Pearl to be the jewel of our work at Yungping. She confessed the Lord and asked for baptism. Up to that time we had baptized none at Yungping. We did not baptize on a mere profession of faith, but only after testing for sincerity and carefully instructing the applicant in its meaning. For the rite of baptism John chose a site at the river. As this would be in full view of the busy market, however, he decided that Small Pearl be baptized very early in the morning, before people were abroad.

There happened, however, to be an early bird, a Chinese woman opposite us, who opened the door that morning to behold a procession issuing from the white man's house across the river.

First came Pastor Kuhn, recognizable by his height and build. Then came Small Pearl. After her Mrs. Kuhn, Miss Kelly, Mrs. Yang, and a string of Chinese—the Christians probably. Pastor Kuhn and Small Pearl entered the river, the others stood on the bank. Then the Pastor took the child and swung her beneath the water! The astonished spectator only watched long enough to assure herself that Small Pearl was allowed to get out alive, when she waddled off to awaken her neighbour to this alarming bit of gossip. In a few hours the whole market buzzed with it. And some of the more courageous ones came over to our house to ask, "What has Small Pearl been doing that she should be treated to such a harsh punishment?" The Christian ritual of baptism was then explained. Alas, not every one chose to be convinced! But some believed.

Small Pearl later became the Mrs. Yang (the schoolmaster's wife) in the story *Nests Above the Abyss*.[1] She was a godly woman, knowing victory in affliction, and was a real soul winner. Our two years in Yungping were worth while if they had given us only Small Pearl.

[1] *Nests Above the Abyss*, C.I.M., 1947.

CHAPTER TEN

THE FORGOTTEN CLOAK

WE had been at Yungping about a year when a letter came from our superintendent, asking John to escort a sick missionary out to Kunming. As I had been suffering from back and head aches it was decided that I go too and consult a doctor.

Travelling overland by mountain chair, usually we stopped at whatever mountain village we came to at dusk, and, as these were very primitive in style, accommodation was indifferent. Dark dusty inns made you glad to get out on the road again the next morning. Our noon meal was purchased at whatever place had anything to eat for sale about midday—rice, vegetables, or perhaps even meat, served on uncovered wooden tables, with chickens and dogs dashing around our feet for scraps which might fall on to the earth from our rice bowls.

I was always glad to get baby Kathryn (due to have her second birthday when we reached Kunming) out of such places and into her mountain chair again. Possibly that was the reason I forgot to pick up my raincoat at one such noon stop and calmly walked off without it! That afternoon we descended a steep hill, on top of which was the village where we had our noon meal. Down, down we went. Mountain tops and ridges were all around us and I was thrilled with the beauty of the scenery. The road dipped into a little valley through which wandered a stream; then we climbed again, but not so high. We skirted the side of the hill for some minutes, then turning a corner came upon Hwang Lien Pu. It was a village comprised of mud or wooden houses on each side of the main road for perhaps half a mile—that was all. Where to find the sleeping place that was least dirty, least smoky, was always our problem, and, having found such, to get our beds in order before nightfall.

It was when we were unpacking and arranging our things that I realized I had forgotten my raincoat and left it at the noon stopping place.

"Oh, John!" I cried rushing out impetuously to lay hold of my tired husband. "I've forgotten my raincoat! It was drizzly this morning, you know, and I had it with me when we stopped for lunch. It is still quite early in the afternoon; do you think you could . . . ?"

"No, I can't!" said John, not waiting for me to finish. He was tired out and still had some dickering with the coolies to go through. They probably wanted "meat money"—a generous tip.

Now I had not intended to ask *him* to go back up that long hill for my coat. We had the young Chinese boy, Ma Fu-yin, with us, and I had thought to offer him some extra money to go after my garment. He was only about twenty years old, and that climb would be nothing to his strong young limbs, bred to these hills. That particular raincoat was more expensive than I had usually purchased, but my father had urged me to get it, since it must last seven years.

"But I can't lose it, John," I argued, probably with heat. "That coat cost money. Someone has got to go back for it. Couldn't Ma Fuh-yin?"

But John himself needed the lad as middleman to placate the chair coolies. "No, I'm not going to send Ma," he answered shortly. And he looked *The Immovable Object*. When he got that expression on his face I knew further talk was useless.

"All right, I'll go myself. Take care of baby," I said and flounced out of the inn and down over the path by which we had first come. I was angry but soothed my conscience by telling myself again the price that had been paid for that coat.

The sun was still warm on my shoulders as I wound my way around the mountain and down to the stream. The steep climb was plainly in view on the opposite hill, and I knew the village where we had stopped at noon was at the top, though out of sight. But I had forgotten how long it took to get even to the foot of the climb.

By now the sun had gone down and in Yunnan there is no long twilight—night comes swiftly on. I began to toil up the steep grade, panting and gasping. Coming down had been easy. I did not realize that it would be so difficult to climb! Dusk turned into dark and still I was struggling up that ascent. I was just tired out and had to sit down to get my breath. Something rustled in the forest above me and I went cold with dread. I

looked up the road I still had to go, and saw that I was merely
at the foot of it. By far the greater part of the climb was yet to
come. Back at the inn at Hwang Lien Pu they would have eaten
supper by now, and I was faint for want of food. I had rushed
off without taking any money. I had no bedding and even if I
managed to reach the village at the top of the hill I could not pay
for lodging or food. It was crazy to go on. I must just eat humble
pie and go back.

"Two years ago," said a Voice in my heart, "you bounced
off just like this, to your sorrow. You promised me then you
wouldn't do it again."

"Yes, Lord, but he would have let my expensive raincoat be
lost!" I defended myself, still sure I was right. Then the Voice of
the Lord was stifled.

All this time my feet were wearily retracing the path to
Hwang Lien Pu. It was so dark by now that I was a bit nervous
at being alone on the wild mountains. As I climbed up on to the
Hwang Lien Pu trail I saw a light ahead; swinging back and
forth. It showed two men coming towards me carrying a lantern.
You can imagine my relief and joy when I found it was John
and Ma Fuh-yin.

"Well, dear, we were coming out to search for you," said
Hubby in a kind voice.

"Thank you, I appreciate that. But I didn't make it. I got too
tired."

"Don't worry, dear. Ma Fuh-yin has promised to go early
tomorrow morning. I'll pay him extra for it. I'm sure he will be
able to get the coat. You must be very hungry."

It was only love and kindness that met me. But I learned a
lesson: *the Lord* was able to move John where I could not. In
future differences of opinion I was to count on that. Besides, I
learned that it is foolish to get excited over a negative answer
from a man who is tired, hungry and harassed. If I had just
waited until John's own problems were settled, of course he
would have been reasonable!

I also learned to beware of precipitate action, to which my
Irish disposition is so prone and which is such a trial to my
deliberate husband. Quick, impulsive action almost always ends
in humiliation and failure.

CHAPTER ELEVEN

A HARD DAY

A YEAR passed, and the way suddenly opened for us to leave Chinese work to junior colleagues (two young ladies returned with us from that trip to Kunming) and enter the Lisu work. As it would be very rough living, Mr. Fraser thought I ought to make a trial trip in to really see conditions before planning to move in permanently. Also there was an unlawful pressure on the new believers to plant opium in the Oak Flat area, where Leila Cooke was alone. (Allyn Cooke was six days north of her in the canyon, teaching and consolidating a new work there.) It was felt that a white man's presence might remind the local feudal laird that he was going beyond the law in this persecution. So John and I prepared to go. Our three-year-old girlie would be left behind in Yungping in charge of our lady colleagues, one of whom was a nurse, so she would receive every care, and we planned to be gone only a month. But it tore my mother-heart to pieces despite full confidence in my fellow-workers, and I walked out of Yungping weeping. You see I was a "softy."

Mountain travel with my strong young capable hubby (he was then only twenty-eight years old) was like another honeymoon.

We took a route which led us up the valley of the Mekong river, which runs parallel to the Salween in north-western Yunnan. At length we came to a hamlet where there was no proper inn, but every traveller stayed in the big adobe farmhouse of the wealthiest inhabitant. It was a sooty dirty place—in fact, we dubbed it "the Dirtiest Inn in the World." We slept upstairs in the granary.

"Tomorrow we climb," said John, "the biggest climb you've ever had! We ought to be on the road by six o'clock if possible, and we climb all morning. But when you reach the top, oh, what a view! You can see the Salween mountains from there! Just think, Belle, tomorrow you will see Lisuland."

It was ten years since I had first heard of the Lisu tribe and felt called to minister to them. How I thrilled at the thought that tomorrow I would see that Alpine land, even though from afar.

But early the next morning I awoke with diarrhoea and an upset stomach.

"Belle!" said John, in a pained voice. "Don't tell me we've got to stay another day in this place!"

"No!" I replied. "If I picked up one germ here by sleeping one night, I'd maybe have two by tomorrow night! We don't stop for this!"

"But it's the hardest climb till we reach the Salween," groaned John. "How can you do it, on an empty stomach and maybe with dysentery beginning?"

"Well, I'm sure I won't improve by an extra day in this dirty place," I argued, "Put me on my horse and then all I have to do is to sit on it!"

And so we began. Up and up, back and forth as the trail zig-zagged upward. About ten in the morning we came to an abandoned tribal hut.

"Here," said John, "let me make you a cup of cocoa. Do you think you could keep it down?"

I was chilled and faint and glad for a few moments' rest from clinging to the animal. Glad for the warmth of the fire John built, and glad when the hot liquid comforted my empty stomach. It stayed down. Then once more on to the animal's back.

The Mekong side of the mountain was heavily wooded, but it was interesting to note the different tree belts. On the lower slopes we had passed through the feathery bamboo, which creaks loudly as the wind stirs its long tubular stems. Then tall pine trees with whispering tops awed us by their height. Still farther up the trees were even greater and older, but so hung with vines, mosses, and ferns that I could not identify their kind. From the great branches these vines fell in loops and festoons perhaps twenty to fifty feet in tangled length. The sun hardly penetrated now and it was getting colder. My promise to sit the horse was not so easy to keep.

Chilled, stiff and weak, my head began to go round and I had to pray for concentration to hold on. John watched me anxiously, cheering me by assurances that the top was not far off now. And finally, with a lunge, my animal pulled himself up over a rocky ledge and stood trembling with relief on a level space—the top of the world! So it looked and felt.

The sun drenched us with a welcome warmth and I was surprised to see that the other side of our mountain was as shorn of tall timber as the Mekong side was shaggy with it. Scrub oak or rhododendron bushes covered its steep sides but did not obscure the scenery, so that far far below us, like a doll's house, we could observe a large farm.

"See, Belle!" said jubilant John, "down there is a big house where we can cook dinner. Keep your courage up. But look!" pointing to the far distance where dark purple peaks undulated along the horizon. "That is Lisuland! Those are the mountains of the Salween gorge. Tomorrow night we ought to be there."

It was a most beautiful panorama and we were tempted to stay and look, but it was already noon and we had no place to cook food until we reached that farmhouse far, far below us. So, with a last longing glance, we began the descent.

It was three in the afternoon before I had my first real meal that day. Luckily this trouble of the morning seemed to have quieted down during my fast. Sunshine and only three o'clock in the afternoon—that was too much for youthful energy. John had been talking to our Chinese farmer-host.

"Say, Belle, you're not going to sleep here, are you? Why, we are not even down the mountain! I've been asking and they say Old Nest, the next village, isn't far away, only about four li after you get down this hill. Let's go on and sleep there! It is a full day from there to the Salween. If we sleep here we won't make the Salween tomorrow."

Now John had misunderstood the garbled Chinese dialect of our host, who was not of pure Chinese blood. John thought he said three or four li when he really said thirty li!—the same sort of thing that had happened when we first went to Tali. If it had been three or four li—a little more than a mile—we would have been there in an hour or so. That is why I readily consented to leave the large comfortable farmhouse and set out for the village of Old Nest.

Once we had fully descended the mountain we found ourselves in the bottom of a deep ravine, winding our way over and around rocks, a noisy stream beside us and no sign of human habitation anywhere. At the end of two hours we were still in the depths of that rocky channel, daylight was fading, and a miserable rain had begun to fall steadily. I had packed my raincoat somewhere in our loads, so it was not long before I was soaked, with the rain streaming off my sun helmet. John was walking while I was riding the animal. Still no sign of Old Nest—or any kind of a nest!

"Belle, I pity you," said repentant Johnny. "Wouldn't you be better off if you were walking here with me? At least your blood would be circulating." It was then six o'clock by my watch.

"I'm too exhausted to walk, dear. Sorry. You're right. I'm cold and stiff and faint. *Where is* Old Nest?"

"I must have misunderstood him, Belle. I'm so sorry. He must have said *san-shih* instead of *san si*. You know how these half-tribal fellows often pronounce it like that. But it has got to be soon. Even thirty li has to end some time!"

Perhaps it was seven o'clock when we finally climbed a hill and arrived at the sprawling village. John led me to a big adobe house that looked prosperous, explained our situation to the owner, and with true Chinese hospitality they invited us in. A huge wood fire was soon blazing on their hearth, and I luxuriated in its warmth while my clothing dried out. A cup of hot tea was soon urged upon me, then hot sugar water with chopped walnuts in it, and a delicious Chinese meal was prepared. In two hours I felt like a different person.

I was the first white woman these people had seen, and the farmhouse soon was crowded with Chinese women and men, looking at me, asking questions, while John took the opportunity to preach the gospel to them.

CHAPTER TWELVE

A GLIMPSE OF STORYBOOK LAND

THE next morning we were up before daylight, and on the road with the first beams of the rising sun. Travelling was hot and tedious; it would have been very hard if the vision seen on the mountain top had not encouraged our hearts. This dusty tortuous way was leading to the Salween—*it had an end*, thus whispered our vision. Our feet stumbled over the rocky path, but our hearts followed the vision and at night time we arrived where the vision had promised—on the bank of the Salween.

The entrance to that part of Lisuland, which was to be our home for so many years, is guarded by a little market town, where three feudal lairds have their Yamen (official residence). It is named Luku, which translated means Six Treasuries. We were entertained by one of these, who took us through his castle and showed us how he had fortified it. That night after supper John whispered to me to go with him for a walk out on the mountainside. As night fell the mountains of the opposite bank of the Salween became jet black towers. Turreted peaks pierced a dark sky spangled with brilliant stars. I was enthralled. "Storybook land!" I gasped. But soon the sombre shadows of the opposite bank of mountains were broken with golden dancing spots of light.

"See that?" whispered John. "Those are Lisu fires! Lisu villages. Belle, dear, you are in Lisuland!"

I can never forget the thrill that went through me.

"*My sheep* wandered through all the mountains, and upon every high hill: yea, my flock was scattered upon all the face of the earth, and none did search or seek after them. My flock became meat to every beast of the field, because there was no shepherd" (Ezek. 34:6, 8). I was looking upon the fires of our Lord's "other sheep." "Other sheep I have, which are not of this fold: them also I must bring" (John 10:16). For unknown centuries they have been forgotten and left prey to every beast of the field, every demon of the devil's host. But now we had come as under-shepherds. Our joy and fellowship with the Great Shepherd at that moment is too sacred to describe, but it was one of life's great moments.

The next day was a series of mountain climbs. By noon we were at a height two thousand feet above the Salween. John pointed to our afternoon road. "We drop down here," he said, "cross the stream at the bottom, climb that set of hairpin turns till level in height with where we are now, go around the brow of that hill, and there is Pine Mountain Village and Leila Cooke."[1]

I looked at the wild chaotic pile of mountains, remembered the many days' journey between here and Chinese civilization from which we had come, heard in memory Mr. Fraser say, "She has not seen another white face for months," and my heart sat at Leila Cooke's feet.

We had wonderful fellowship together. The second day after our arrival, Mark of Goomoo with his two comrades and his challenging story arrived. (This is told in *Nests Above the Abyss*.) By the third or fourth morning John was feeling the need of exercise.

"I think I'll just go out and help those fellows work the garden," he said to me, disappearing through the door. Leila Cooke and I were inside busy about something, when suddenly we heard laughter, then peals of laughter, then gales of it. Leila got up, went to the door and looked out.

"Well," she exclaimed, "I was told there was a second side to John Kuhn that few people get to see, but I didn't believe it. Now I know." I went and looked over her shoulder. Two Lisu boys had been hoeing the rough mountainside preparatory to planting a garden. Now they were rolling on the ground holding their sides with laughter. John, who could not yet speak Lisu so could not yet talk to them, had taken the hoe. They had looked astonished but yielded the implement at his request. Solemnly he raised it, gave it a mighty whirl, and brought it down heavily, just missing the clod of earth aimed at. At first their laughter was covert, but when his pantomime made it obvious that he was

[1] Mrs. A. B. Cooke, author of *Honey Two of Lisuland* and *Fish Four*.

just clowning for their benefit, their delight knew no bounds. From that day he became Big Brother, beloved and adored.

Leila Cooke was with us only long enough to explain a certain persecution the church was undergoing because they refused to plant opium. Then she left us to rejoin her husband who was in the Luda district, six days' journey to the north. Moses, a tribesman, who spoke Chinese, was our interpreter.

Before she departed Leila Cooke said to me (as if it were a casual matter), "Oh, by the way, Moses' wife is expecting, you know. I promised to help her. But if the baby comes before I return you'll have to be in charge, I suppose."

"Oh!" I cried aghast, "I couldn't! I've never seen such a thing and I've had no training and . . ."

"I haven't had training either," she replied, "but there is nobody else to help her! A Lisu woman might be obtained but they are not clean, you know. You and I at least understand hygiene. And as for not having seen a birth—you've had a baby yourself, haven't you?"

"Yes," I gasped. "But I—er—wasn't taking note of the procedure."

"Well, there are some books on obstetrics in the lower shelf," Leila said, indicating her bookcase. "And to comfort you—none of her other babies have lived. They were all still-born. So if this one is also, you need not feel it was your fault. But I wish for Moses' sake this one could live. He would so love to have a child. . . . Well, goodbye. We'll pray for one another!" And off she went.

I cannot describe my feelings. Remember I am a "softy." The very idea of being responsible for a birth gave me cold chills. I seized the obstetric books and they were full of incidents of abnormal cases. The more I read the more nightmares I got! And it was dear Moses' wife and baby!

This Moses was the Fish Four of the moving story written by Leila Cooke. I had met him before and been deeply impressed. His breadth of brow betokened the unusual intellect he possessed, but he was so humble and modest, always shrinking into the background. I had come to love him dearly in the Lord. There was an atmosphere of *rest* about him, the serene peace of a life abandoned to the Lord and governed by Him. Yet he was a born leader of men. When he conducted the singing in church there was a grace of movement and a power to inspire that I have seldom seen equalled.

Mrs. Cooke had told me how the white people in Shanghai had been thrilled with him and wanted to give him gifts, white cambric shirts among other things. "We feared that he might be spoiled before he got back to these rough hills," she continued, "but to our relief he went right into native homespun clothes and we've never seen a sign of those cambric shirts. I've sometimes wondered what he has done with them."

A few days after she left us, there was a baptismal service at Pine Mountain and Moses, as native pastor, officiated. When he went down into the pool, he stood a moment and rolled up his sleeves. There under the navy blue homespun was a fine cambric cuff. Hastily he turned it back up and under. But I had seen it. He was wearing his Western finery, but where it would not show, and his poorer Lisu brethren would never be moved to envy by it.

Do you wonder why we loved Moses? And was I to be the one, by bungling ignorance, to cost him another child? The thought did not help to steady my nerves. Vainly I hoped the birth would be postponed until Mrs. Cooke got back.

She had been gone perhaps ten days, when Moses came to me. "Big Sister," he said, "Grace is having stomach ache. Would you kindly come and see her?" Quickly I went up to their shanty, which stood on the slope just above ours. His wife Grace was crouched in the far corner of the room. She looked like a wild animal cornered by the inescapable, and she would obey no advice of mine! I gave all the medical counsel which had been given to me. She would act on none of it. She would not even talk with me.

"Well, we will get things sterilized and arranged, Moses," I said, my heart beating quickly with excitement. "I have studied the medical books and we must prepare so-and-so and so-and-so," naming off the items. "Also we think the baby does better if it sleeps by itself." I added this doubtfully, for I knew the Lisu did not agree with us in this.

"I would like my baby brought up like your babies," he said quickly. "Would this basket do for a baby bed?" It was just right. With great joy I got some materials Leila Cooke had left at my disposal, and we fixed the basket up very prettily. Moses, usually so calm and deliberate, was obviously stirred and excited. All that day we waited and nothing happened. I went to bed with my clothes on, expecting an early call, but none came. Grace was still where I first saw her. She would not get up, she would not walk or exercise, she just crouched in the corner. As the day progressed Moses got anxious—I could see it in his eyes. As for me, mine were nearly inflamed from poring over the medical books! There was instruction as to preparation, and advice as to reception and after birth care, but not a word on what to do to induce labour.

By late afternoon the concern in Moses' eyes haunted me. He never lost his slow serene movements, but his eyes belied that calm behaviour. "Isn't there a medicine you can give her to speed it up, Ma-ma?" he asked.

Pray? I had prayed until I was nearly exhausted. John did not know any more than I did about what to do. But from somewhere in the past I thought I remembered somebody saying something about using quinine.

"There is a medicine I think I heard once that someone advised. But oh, Moses, I can't be sure! No book tells me either. If it was the wrong medicine it might kill her! And I don't know the dosage."

"I'm willing to try it," said the poor fellow, his eyes pleading for help.

"Oh, Moses, you trust me too much. I'm not *sure* I heard rightly." I was in an agony of doubt. "I tell you, let us pray about it. You go back and pray and I will stay here and pray. After ten minutes come back and we'll see how the Lord has led us."

How I pleaded that God would not let me make a mistake! But gradually the conviction came that I should try quinine in small doses. When Moses returned I asked him, "What do you think?"

"I think we should try that medicine, Ma-ma."

"I feel the same. All right, here it is. Now Moses, we are going to give her one two-grain pill every half-hour. You watch carefully. If you see any new development call me immediately." And with that, for the second night I lay down in my clothes.

It was not yet midnight when a knock came at our door. I was up in a moment. It was Moses.

"Please come, Ma-ma."

I don't know how I got up that dark mountainside. I was shaking from head to foot. Had I killed her? She was lying down this time and I turned my flashlight upon her. In another moment a little one was in our hands.

"It's dead," said Moses mournfully, when a piercing wail rent the air!

God uses the foolish things of the earth veritably and had been merciful to this inexperienced "nurse." A lovely baby girl, whom they named Esther, was soon clean and rosy, daintily wrapped up in her wee bed, sleeping peacefully.

For the first and only time I saw Moses excited. His eyes shone like stars for joy. He ministered to the baby much more than her mother, and with such a loving tenderness and lingering over her, that it brought the tears to my eyes. No sleep for him— joy was his food and drink. He spent the hours while baby slept, writing letters to all his friends and relatives. He just wanted to tell *everybody* that this baby had lived.

The afternoon of the second day he came to me with trouble in his eyes.

"Do you have any tinned milk, Ma-ma?" he asked. "I'd like to buy some. Baby Esther's mother cannot feed our child."

I stared at him a moment, then pulled my face straight.

"I will gladly sell you milk, Moses," I said, "but it is usual for the mother not to start feeding the baby until the third day."

Oh, what a relief! Once more life was a joy, and he turned round to speed back to his young Madonna with this wonderful news. Baby Esther grew chubby and strong.

She was not yet a month old, however, before a runner came in from Allyn Cooke in the north. It contained a message something like this: "If Moses' baby has been born, please ask him to come up and help us here for three months. The work is spreading so—we need him."

"Oh," I cried to John, "how cruel to ask Moses to leave just now! Three months? Why, he will miss all the first baby awakenings, the first smile, the first laugh. Oh, I *can't* deliver this message."

But as it turned out, I was the one who had to do it, after all. We were standing in the main room of our shanty, and through the open door the beautiful snow-clad peaks of the opposite bank of the Salween jutted up into the blue, blue sky. As I delivered the message Moses gave me one startled look, then he turned and gazed at those steadfast sparkling peaks. Obviously Moses was speaking in his heart with his Lord. For, as I watched, his face cleared and was suffused with peace. Turning to me he said quietly, "I will go if the Lord wants me to go." It had been but a short struggle. The one big "yes" of utter consecration had been said some years before, so that the further surrender of each new gift or joy from Him did not consume much time or wrestling.

I felt I was standing on holy ground, and I prayed within my heart, "Lord, this is just one Lisu. If his race can produce such devotion, wilt Thou take my life and use it in teaching them of Thee?"

CHAPTER THIRTEEN

A PARTING THAT DID NOT PART

THE month we had promised to stay soon drew to its close. But the opium persecution affair was not yet settled. The Lisu church desired that John stay on for a few more weeks. He wanted to stay on too, but I had promised the girls that I would be back in about a month. It was already past that and there was no way to telegraph them of delay. Neither could we tell when the opium business would be settled. As a matter of fact, John did not get back until June. So I felt I must return to Yungping and relieve the young missionaries of my work so that they could pursue their studies.

It was decided that Ma Fu-yin go with me. He was an attractive Christian Chinese lad of about twenty who had come with us and consented happily to be my escort back. There was a shorter route, John thought, than the one by way of Old Nest village, but I would still have to cross the mountains. Few used that road, and I believe I am the only white woman who has ever been over it. It crossed directly to the Mekong valley. Chinese market towns dot that road, so it was easy to get food and lodging. I rode Jasper, a wily old mule lent to us by Mr. Fraser.

John and I will never forget that parting. My heart was torn between husband and child. I did not like to leave John, although our Lisu friends would feed him well and care for him. At the same time I had never before been separated from Kathy, and I could hardly wait to get back to her. John did not like to see me go either, so he decided to ride with me to the top of Place-of-Action mountain, which he reckoned would be about half-way along my first day's journey.

The scenery was indescribably gorgeous. Higher up the mountain than Place-of-Action village was the village of Golden Bamboo, where we had many Christians, so we had slept there the night before and climbed from there. The road went hairpinning back and forth, back and forth, each rise in altitude giving a farther glimpse of mountain peaks behind the great summits which banked the canyon. I felt we were climbing to the top of the world—mountain-tops like the waves of the sea spread out in all directions, but the sea-troughs were abysses of great depth. My heart trembled even as it thrilled.

Then the path left the banks of the Salween and began to travel into one of the tributary rivers but it still ascended. It was a mere cow path, which necessitated our going single file. At one place we skirted a great rocky knoll and jutted out over nothing! I closed my eyes lest the drop at the side of the path should unsteady me, for it would be a fearful plunge over that edge!

Till almost noon we rode, then the path seemed to have reached the top of the range, and looked to be level far on ahead. John reined in his horse. "Well, Belle, I guess we part here," he said. A lump was in my throat. I must go on alone now, and leave him alone.

Now when I have to face a separation which is painful I like to get it over with quickly. So when John called Ma Fu-yin and the Lisu carriers together for a parting prayer, I was hoping he would make it short! But not so Johnny. His disposition is quite different. Propriety is very important to him and to hurry through such a separation is a shallow performance not worthy of a real Christian. So, after a lengthy prayer, he raised his voice and began to sing,

> "God be with you till we meet again,
> By His counsels guide, uphold you,
> With His sheep securely fold you,
> God be with you. . . ."

Now singing is just the last straw, emotionally, to me. The camel's back breaks every time. So when he plaintively continued,

> "Till we me-ee-et—Till we me-et
> Till we meet at Jesus' feet,"

visions of all the awful things that might happen to dear Hubby in that canyon before I saw him again harrowed me until I felt I could not stand it. But John inexorably went on,

> "Till we me-ee. . . ."

I opened my eyes. "*Please* stop it," I was going to say, when I caught sight of a tail whisking around the corner. There was another objector—Jasper had jerked his head loose from Ma Fu-yin who, with closed eyes, was valiantly trying to follow the song, with which he was not too familiar. When I saw Jasper, his hind legs and tail were waving a gay farewell. Back down over the trail we had just come raced the animal, driving in front of him John's mount also. John never did get this "me-ee-et" finished. I screamed, and Ma Fu-yin, feeling a jerk on his hand, came back to earth, picked up his heels, and started off in chase of Jasper and the other horse!

But this was a delightful game to the mule. Down hill the whole way, you know, and such a narrow road that Ma Fu-yin could find no short cut to steer him off! Also such an untravelled road that there was nobody at all to stop him en route. Jasper and the horse raced gaily around sharp corners, Ma Fu-yin after them, legs and arms flying like a windmill. Out of sight of his pursuer Jasper would stop to nibble the delicious green grasses richly banking the wild path. As the human windmill turned the corner and came into view, off went the two animals again. Left horseless on that high trail, we waited for a while, then decided to walk together back down the trail, hoping against hope to meet Ma Fu-yin with a subdued and repentant Jasper in tow. No such good fortune! Hour after hour we plodded on foot back over the way we had ridden. Finally we came again to the banks of the Salween, and far down almost to Golden Bamboo Village we beheld Ma Fu-yin with Jasper in tow at last. But it was now too late in the day to proceed. That night we slept in the same place from which we had left that morning.

"Now don't you think it is the Lord trying to persuade you to stay with me?" suggested Hubby hopefully the next morning.

"No," said his stubborn spouse, "I think it is a warning to you not to indulge in such long-drawn out partings!"

This time John decided not to escort me, but he took a seat on a big stone by the side of the road. And as our party ascended back and forth over the hairpin turns, he became smaller and smaller, until he looked the size of a pin-head, still waving his handkerchief.

The rest of that day's journey was lonely but grand. At the very top of the range we came upon a little sun-kissed meadow where gurgled a sparkling clean brook, a wonderful place for a camp. But we pressed on. Dusk was falling before we even began to descend. And finally I got off the weary mule and stumbled down the mountain-side, with only pale moonlight to show the trail. We stopped for the night at the first village.

The next day's journey was most pleasant. The road wound through rice fields beginning to show their emerald green, and often by the banks of the blue Mekong river.

Late that afternoon we came to a small market town beside the first bridge which we had seen. Here there was a small inn with a stable in the inner courtyard. Ma Fu-yin came to me, "Szu-mu," he said, "I don't think that stable will keep this mule inside. He is devilish wise, you know. I've never met such an animal, and I have misgivings about what he'll do tonight."

The owner of the place seemed to be a woman. "Da-ma" (great mother), I said to her, "Haven't you a door for that stable? I fear our mule will get out if you haven't."

"Get out of my stable? Nonsense," she said, "it has bars that are put across. Animals stay there all the time—nothing ever gets out."

"But our mule is old and wise. I fear those bars won't hold him. Can't you help us make it more secure?"

"No need, no need," she said confidently. "I'll guarantee he'll not get out if you put the bars down."

About three o'clock the next morning I was awakened by a most fearful racket downstairs. An excited voice was swearing in a high pitched tone. Something big was being whacked! It sounded like an elephant in a china shop. Suddenly a shrill neigh awoke my suspicions. I sat up in bed and called out, "Ma Fu-yin!" Soon his slender form appeared in my doorway but he was shaking with suppressed laughter. Chinese oaths and execrations continued, mingled with whacks, from below.

"It was Jasper!" whispered Ma Fu-yin. "During the night he lifted the stable bars off with his nose, strode out into the court-yard, sniffed Da-ma's big pan of beancurd which she had made to sell on the market today. He went into her kitchen and had eaten about half of it before she woke up and found him!"

It was an irate innkeeper that said goodbye to us after breakfast.

But naughty as Jasper was, I never forgot that that old mule had done me one great favour. Thereafter, whenever a painful and prolonged parting was in prospect I had only to say pleadingly, "John, please! Remember Jasper!"

CHAPTER FOURTEEN

THE THING WITH THE STUFF IN IT

IT was December (1934) before we were finally able to move into Lisuland as a family. It was quite an undertaking. At Pine Mountain almost the only vegetable that could be purchased was corn. Sometimes a salt merchant came around, rice could be bought, and chickens were frequently obtainable. Eggs we traded for medicine—an egg for a pill—not evaluating the size of the pill or the age of the egg! But flour, sugar, tinned milk and goods we must bring in. Clothes and bedding must also be packed for horse loads, as well as kerosene for light, tools for building, books and medicine. The money used in the canyon was silver, which weighed heavily if you were taking in enough for several months' living expenses. We would need to hire carriers, also servants, since water had to be carried from well to house. Besides, the nearest mail box was a day's journey away. All in all we found ourselves with eleven pack horses. John decided that the easiest route for pack animals was via Old Nest village again.

So we started out. The weather was beautiful—clear blue skies with golden sunshine and just enough nip in the air to stimulate exercise and appetite.

Kathryn being with us, she and I rode in a sedan chair while John rode Jasper. Where it was too steep for the porters to carry baby and me together, I got out and rode the mule and John walked.

It was pleasant travelling up the beautiful Mekong valley, but eventually, of course, we came to "The Dirtiest Inn in the World." We had a merry time in that sooty farmhouse. Cooped up all day long in the chair, Kathryn was all activity as soon as we got out. She was three years old and into everything. Now much can be washed off with cold water, but soot! To get hot water, we had to heat it in a grimy pot over an open wood fire on the floor or in the courtyard. Our patience was tried to the breaking point. We longed for nightfall in order to put Kathryn to bed, and then we tried to get everything packed up and breakfast cooked before we woke her in the morning, so that she would not look quite like a chimney sweep by the time we started.

At length we were ready; horses' loads were lined up waiting to have the animals led under them. We had finished breakfast and I had saved some warm water to give Kathryn a last hand wash before I put her in the chair. For myself, I despaired of ever starting out clean. The place was such a junk shop and the low ceilings so festooned with sooty cobwebs, I had only to turn round and something was sure to brush a black mark against my cheek, or my skirt, or my hands. Unknown to me, John had found it as irritating as I had, but he had prepared some hot water in a different room and made up his mind to have a wash *just* before setting out.

Muleteers, chair porters, Kathryn and I were all ready to leave, but where was John? We usually had prayer together before setting out.

"John," I called. "Hurry up! We're all waiting for you." No answer. Where could he be? I was about to call again, when he emerged from a side room beaming with amiability.

"See, Belle," he said, glowing with success, and holding out two spotless palms for my admiration. "At least I'm clean when I leave."

"What on earth!" He had turned over his newly washed hands and there, behold, a black streak of soot across the back of one! He must have brushed against something as he came out the door! "Would you look at that," he said, disgusted. "What a place! Well, I'll . . ." and he began peering into this load and that one. "Belle, where is the thing with the stuff in it?"

I stood, knitting my brow, trying to think what he meant.

But my silence he interpreted as non-cooperation. "Where's that thing with the stuff in it?" He shot the question at me again. The muleteers could not understand English (would it have helped if they could?) but they knew that something concerning the loads had displeased their sunny-tempered master, and had a feeling that it would be wise to appear industrious at this moment, so they began pulling at ropes and poking at the horses with an anxious manner. Only I stood there appearing to be idle; in reality I was scurrying around mentally trying to guess what John was hunting for.

"Belle!" he protested. "Why don't you help a fellow? You stand there gaping—*Where's that thing with the stuff in it?*"

Then my indignation broke. "I defy anyone in this universe to help you, John Kuhn, when you use such ambiguous language. *A thing with the stuff in it?* Why everywhere I look," indicating the eleven horse loads, "everywhere I look there are *things* with *stuff* in them!"

But my retort was lost. He was half buried in the depths of one basket, from which he emerged at last, smiling and calm, holding up a tube of hand cream. "Don't get excited, dear," he said soothingly, "I just thought this would take the soot mark off. I'm ready now."

The muleteers, seeing that the sun was shining again, straightened up with relief and began to call the animals forward. And Daddy led us in prayer for protection on the road that day.

As we began to climb a particularly difficult and arduous part of the ascent I began to picture to John the scene of the morning, mimicking his question until its unreasonableness dawned upon him. Then he began to laugh—laugh until he could hardly climb. (You see, there is more than one way of rubbing a thing in!) So it has become another of our family jokes. In fact for twelve years now it has helped us over the small crises of life when something quickly needed is difficult to lay hands on. If one of us roars, "The thing with the stuff in it?" then in the midst of subsequent laughter a more accurate description speedily follows.

CHAPTER FIFTEEN

FURLOUGH WITHOUT BAGGAGE (1936)

THEN followed sixteen months of happy work in Lisuland, wherein memories include the building of our shanty, "Home of Grace." John always hoped he would not be asked to build a house on the mission field, but when it fell to his lot he built it so strong that it stood well for some twenty years, in fact until the Communists tore it down.

Now as we started on our first furlough we sailed from Shanghai on the *President McKinley*. We had the joy of fellowship with a missionary family in the cabin next to us, and we had prayer together daily in our cabin.

On one of these occasions, when we had just finished and were in the act of getting off our knees, a fellow passenger, dashing merrily down the corridor, mistook our cabin for his own, and barged in. The poor man was not only surprised, he was petrified! When he so suddenly arrived in our midst we were neither on our knees, nor as yet upright; we were half-way up, groping in the air. He looked as if he thought he had landed in a cell of an insane asylum, and his face so clearly revealed his thoughts that we fell back in our chairs convulsed with laughter.

In those days ocean liners held a Hard Time Party once during the voyage. It was announced for the evening meal one day, and we were all informed by the steward that we would not be served dinner unless we appeared in costume. He looked at the two C.I.M. missionary families as he said this, thinking possibly that people who had a prayer meeting every day would be too long faced for fun making. We did not undeceive him.

It was John's costume I remember best. Believe it or not, he dressed up as a bold pirate in a sleeveless waistcoat and a pair of shorts with a gay sash round the middle. Into this was stuck a hunting knife. A red bandana tied round his head was splashed with mercurochrome. He blackened hollows under his eyes with a burnt cork and produced streaks of soot with the same on cheeks, shoulders and legs. Mercurochrome supplied more gory-looking gashes for neck and limbs—his hair under the bandana was combed down over his eyes. Being big, muscular, and hairy, he was a fearsome sight. I had pulled my hair back tight from my face and did it up in a teapot handle, in imitation of Maggie Jiggs. With long skirts to the floor I looked the part. Together we sailed into the dining-room, a trifle late, and solemnly faced the steward. He had prided himself on being able to identify every-body. We stood there, John scowling in good pirate fashion, and I looking down the length of my nose at him. The steward was dumbfounded. Giggles came from those already seated. He looked around to see who was yet missing to help him catch a clue, but several tables were vacant. He could not guess our identity for the life of him. Finally he had to ask who we were!

As we passed between tables, one of the men called out, "You take first prize, sir!" And when it got noised abroad that the ferocious pirate was the supposedly long-faced missionary, one of the other men guests got up and came to John and said, "Con-gratulations! You're a good sport."

If the rest of the evening had been games and good fun it would have been a happy evening. But when dinner was over drinking began; dancing and card games soon drove us to our cabin, so we were not present when the prizes were awarded.

Our ship did not dock at Vancouver, where my father and brother lived. The destination was Seattle. So we had to dis-embark at Victoria and take a coastal steamer from there to Vancouver. John was given baggage tickets to see to the transfer of our luggage from the one ship to the other. We were not prepared, however, for the wonderful reception that the Mission friends in Victoria gave us. Since the local boat was not leaving immediately, they had planned a trip for us to Buchard's Sunken Gardens. Just to see homeland shores was thrilling enough; but the excitement of meeting everybody eclipsed everything else.

It was only after the ship to Vancouver was actually pulling out of Victoria harbour that John suddenly clapped his hands on his pocket—then with chagrin he pulled out the baggage tickets and held them up to me. "Belle, look! I completely forgot about them!"

"Oh, John!" That meant we had nothing but what we stood up in—not even an overnight case!

A hasty interview with the purser brought comfort. We could wire for our things to be forwarded to us on the next ship. That night, amidst much laughter, our friends brought us night clothes to sleep in! And only a few days later our trunks came safely to hand.

All the way from Lisuland to Vancouver we had experienced the covering of His hand!

That arrival in Vancouver was memorable. My father and brother were at the dock; somehow I had not expected so many of my girl friends also to be there. But there they were! It was exciting to lead John up to them and make him guess from my previous descriptions just who was who. And he did not make many mistakes.

Kathryn monopolized Grandpa. We had carefully built up a story around him, telling of the peppermint candy that always hid in his pockets, and so on. We hoped she would not be strange with him, and she wasn't. In fact she clung to him so that he could go nowhere without her.

We were in Vancouver for about three weeks and then crossed the border into the United States to attend The Firs Bible and Missionary Conference at Bellingham, Washington State. This was the conference where I first had offered my life for foreign service, and I did want my friends there to get to know John.

This year of 1936 the chief speakers were Dr. Lewis Sperry Chafer, Mr. L. E. Maxwell of Prairie Bible Institute, Dr. John G. Mitchell and Miss Frances Brook. All four left an imprint on our lives that was permanent, as those who have read our letters can easily discern.

Among the many dear saints of the Lord who attended that conference were Mr. and Mrs. Eastman. They lived on Orcas Island in Puget Sound, a favourite summer resort. There they had built a few summer cottages as an investment. But one of these they had dedicated to the Lord to be loaned to missionaries who needed rest. When they offered it to us, urging us to come at the end of the conference, we promised to pray about it.

I was still underweight, due to a hard bout of sickness before furlough. Also I was highly strung and worn after eight years of service on the field. I needed quietly to get away from even the dear excitement of visiting old friends. John, who takes life more calmly, was in no such need. He liked to be on the go, loved to visit, did not require a full night's sleep, and even could stand lengthening his day till midnight. Yet we did not like to separate—that was not any fun either. But it was obvious that I must get where I could sleep and relax. So it came about that August, 1936 saw us established in a couple of rooms over a garage in Orcas Island. A nearby cabin in the woods housed Grandpa Miller, who could not bear to be parted from us.

It proved to be a beautiful little island, with a permanent farming community. In fact, right behind us was a small farm where a middle-aged couple had built a two-roomed cabin. As the sale of produce from their farm was bringing in sufficient money, they were adding a third room about the time of our arrival.

I was ordered to sleep late every morning, to try to build up physically. But healthy John found time hanging heavy on his hands. Grandpa liked to fish, but that did not solve John's need for exercise. Finally one morning he announced, "There is an old man next door roofing a side wing of his cabin. He seems to be all alone, and I wonder if he wouldn't like help. I'm going to offer. I just must get some physical work, or I'll get fat and lazy. Come on, Grandpa, you're good for a few shingles and nails, aren't you?"

Grandpa, who thought the world of his son-in-law, could not deny it. So that morning saw the short fat figure and the tall muscular one approach the new wing where our neighbour was perched on the rafters, nails in his mouth, shingles and hammer in his hands.

"Hi there!" called out John. "Want any help? We'd be glad to come up and assist you!"

Amazed, our neighbour could hardly believe that here were volunteer workmen who wanted no pay.

"Well, I take that as exceedingly kind! But you ought to be told that it is pretty hot up here on the roof."

"Oh, that's O.K.," said John. "A good sweat is healthy. How about our getting to work now? Can you find an extra hammer, do you think?"

So it came about that, lying on my bed in the flat, along with the call of the sea birds which drifted in through the open windows, I could hear the rat-a-tat-tat of two or three hammers on the Loomis' roof behind us. Five-year-old Kathryn was, of course, with the working contingent! Playing house with broken shingles and wandering with Grandma Loomis through her vegetable garden, she was content. The old couple were simply thrilled with their wageless labourers! They kept up a steady stream of gifts from their garden. Squash, beans, cucumbers, just whatever they had, found its way to our kitchen.

More than that, when John went to the corner grocery to buy some coffee, the proprietor beamed on him. "Aren't you the missionary who is working for Grandpa Loomis? We hear you're going to preach for Mr. Eastman Sunday night. Well, we're coming. Guess you'll have a pretty good crowd! Your reputation has sort of got around the island. A missionary working like that and for nothing, you know!"

So the heart of the island opened to us. We were invited to this farmstead and to that; and we formed friendships that lasted for years. In fact I believe that on Orcas Island there are some who still pray for the Kuhn family and the Lisu tribe.

So once again we found that the Lord's way is the happy way. John's was a blessed surrender for my health's sake, and brought joy and happiness to many more beside himself.

CHAPTER SIXTEEN

HOME TOWN

WITH strength renewed we left the Pacific northwest for a visit to Daddy's home town, Manheim, Pennsylvania. After the train sped across the three thousand intervening miles, we finally saw the rolling farmlands that gave us the signal that we were nearing our station, Lancaster. We all got excited. It was ten years since Daddy had sailed for China and this was his first return home. And although I had visited his sister at one time, this was my first visit as an in-law belonging to the family!

Who would be at the station to meet us?

John's parents were both dead, but he had two half-brothers, Bill and Jim, who still lived there with Aunt Annie and Uncle Anton. And we were to stay there too. Then there was John's "spiritual mother," Mrs. John Kready. John's own mother had died when he was three years old and dear Mrs. Kready had taken him on her heart to pray him into the Kingdom; then later she stood behind him in prayer as he went down to God's front line of battle in China. Already Mother Kready's letters and spiritual premonitions of our needs had made a great impression on me. Would she be at the station?

I was also most anxious to meet a certain young bookkeeper named Mary Zimmerman. She had written to me while we were still in China, asking permission to duplicate our monthly prayer letters and include them in a little periodical she compiled each month called *The Triangle*. At the time she wrote I had never met her or heard of her. But I had been praying to the Lord about our letters. I had felt I should write once a month to people who really prayed for the work—but it would cost too much to post a monthly letter to many people directly from China. So I had prayed, "Lord, if you want this letter multiplied you will have to find the way." About six months or a year later, there had come this request. At that time *The Triangle* went to only about one hundred people; but still that meant one hundred to pray for the Lisu! I was very grateful, and now I questioned, "Will Mary be at the train to meet us?"

There were others too, of whom John had spoken often and whose faces I had seen in snapshots only. Would I recognize them now? But here the train was pulling to a stop and we must not forget our baggage the second time. In another minute we were out on the platform and surrounded with people! I could hear John's voice joyously naming them. "Aunt Annie! Brother Bill! Brother Jim! Mother Kready!"

Then almost immediately a young woman in a Mennonite cap edged forward and said, "I'm Mary Zimmerman. Could you speak for me at a meeting on the 18th?" I gasped; my head was going round with all the excitement. But how often I have chuckled over that first meeting with Mary! She had only her noon hour for time off, of course, and it is her remarkable ability to make every moment count which has enabled her to do the work of several people. She wanted me to speak to her prayer group, knowing that it would do much for me as well as for them.

"Why yes, I'd be glad to speak," I replied to her.

"Good. I'll 'leave' you know the details and arrange transportation for you later," she added, with that perfect attention to business detail which blesses her friends. And that was also my introduction to the quaint Pennsylvania Dutch way of putting things. It was all a part of John's Home Town.

Finally we were escorted into Brother Bill's car, and whirled off for Manheim. Lancaster County, with its green hills and beautifully kept farmhouses and barns, is one of the lush spots of America. John was thrilled, glancing from side to side of the road, recognizing landmarks and chatting with the relatives, sometimes trying to point out places to me.

Then we were in the town itself. The first impression to me, who had been brought up in the wide open spaces of western lands, was of the houses opening right off the street and closely packed together. In the west almost everybody had a front garden, a back yard and side yards; each home was a unit by itself. But here they were built two together like Siamese twins. To have your front doorstep opening right on to the street gave me the quaint feeling of being in medieval Germany. Everything was other-worldish, and the sight of people on the street in Mennonite costume increased my impression that I had walked into the pages of a story-book.

The car drove up to one of these double houses and Aunt Annie called out that we were *home*! Everything was immaculately clean. Annie and Anton, as their nephews called them, had no children, and were the indefatigable, industrious type. And soon we were called down to supper and I was introduced to Pennsylvania Dutch hospitality! There were three or four different kinds of pie on the table at the same time, and so on.

In my innocence, the first time I offered to help with the housework, I was dubiously given the hanging up of the laundry. I had no more than a line full up when one of the family asked, horrified, "Isobel, did nobody ever teach you how to hang up clothes?" Quickly they hauled everything off that I had hung up, lest the neighbours discover that John's wife did not know any better than that! No, no one had ever taught me that there was an Emily Post set of rules for hanging out clothes—so you see I had to learn from the bottom up. John's wife might do as a public speaker or even as a missionary author, but as far as the practical things of life were concerned—well, it was easy to see that I was not brought up in Manheim! On the whole they were very indulgent with me.

Manheim was then a town of about four thousand inhabitants. John had been born there, but the Kuhn homestead now belonged to an older brother of John's father. Of course we went around to see it and then to inspect the old swimming hole at the end of the street. From there to the Hershey Machine and Foundry Company, where John had worked for a year in order to earn money to start his studies at Moody Bible Institute. And then off we went to see the school that John had attended. From there down Main Street, dropping in at the drug store so that I might meet some distant relatives of the Kuhn family, fine Christian people.

On down Main Street to the corner of the square. "Here is where everybody comes on Saturday night," explained John. "People drive in from the country round to do their shopping, and everywhere there is lively chatter. Sister Kathryn and I used to hold open-air services here when we were home from Moody. I've preached many a time at the corner there."

Near the Square was the home of a fine Christian business man who helped John first at Moody Bible Institute and then through all the years he was a missionary in China. He was a real lover of the Lord Jesus Christ, and his keen business brain was used in his Christian living and giving until his Home-call. It was a privilege to discuss problems with him and watch "sanctified common sense" go into action.

There was yet another place on the town square which demanded a visit from us. That was the bank. Here was deposited the cash legacy which came to John on his father's death. It was a nice little nest egg. We had recently been reading C. T. Studd's Life and it had made a real impression on us. You remember that Studd gave away his entire fortune. John was for doing the same, but I felt we should be careful not to rush into such action.

I reminded John of the need of my father, who was an earnest Christian and a deacon in the church, but who had no compunctions about going into debt, even running up a charge account when he had not an income sufficient to pay for it. He was always most optimistically expecting that something would "turn up." To my dear husband's everlasting credit be it said that in accord with the scriptural challenge of 1 Timothy 5:8, the first cheques that were drawn on his legacy wiped out my father's indebtedness. It amounted to nearly five hundred dollars. As for the remainder, we offered it to the Lord on our knees, and then arose expecting Him to tell us where it should be given. It was a thrillingly sweet adventure to watch His finger pointing. One hundred was given to an earnest young missionary working on the border of Russia; another hundred to help outfit a new worker for Africa; another to enable a fine Christian girl to finish at Prairie Bible Institute; another to send a missionary to South America; and more hundreds to enable a Manheim girl to go to Moody Bible Institute. This latter lassie from John's own home town met and married a keen soul-winner at M.B.I. and together they have been burning and shining lights for the Lord in Central America for many years.

As for us, we lacked nothing. Without a car, friends offered this help so that we never lacked transportation. Speaking engagements were piling up and a generous friend provided my "platform clothes." John was cared for by others, and Kathryn was sent to kindergarten by still others.

These provisions were all the more astounding because there in Manheim everybody must have heard the amount Father Kuhn left to his children. We had told no one what John meant to do with his share, not even our brothers and sisters, so our friends could not have thought that we were financially pinched or lacking. It was just the Lord that prompted them to care for our needs, as He had prompted us to meet the needs of His other children in other parts of the world.

"God is no man's debtor," said one of Hudson Taylor's friends to him, and we have proved it true.

Now as one sits back and views the small town community, removed by space and over a period of some thirty years, "*the inheritance of saints*" is the most outstanding impression. Gradually I have come to see that, with my husband, I have gained a rich portion of this great inheritance of saints.

CHAPTER SEVENTEEN

THE TICKLISH QUESTION

THE time was now approaching when our little daughter must enter school, and we ourselves were due to return to the field.

How can the child of missionaries, especially pioneer missionaries working on a far and primitive field, get an education?

This is *the* most ticklish of all missionary problems, and feelings run deep and warm on the subject.

To keep a child alone among adults, especially one of Kathy's gregarious disposition, was a positive cruelty. The way she would simply tremble with delight at the idea of playmates used to stab my heart. To let her continue to play with the Lisu children was also out of the question. I had had a fellow-worker, a child of the Mission, once draw me aside and warn me, with tears in her eyes, not to expose my child to the immoral things she might see and hear from native playmates. "I'd give anything if I could wipe out some of my childhood memories," this girl said to me. "My parents were good missionaries, but they thought if they put 'the work' first, God would take care of their children." (After all, what is *the* work—God's work—for a young mother?) God does not always work miracles to deliver us from the consequences of our mistakes. The wife of our General Director had also solemnly warned me along this line shortly after I arrived in China. So this was the second warning.

I felt that this was the voice of the Lord to me; especially as I had already felt that before God I was surely more responsible for the souls that I brought into existence than for those that someone else did! And now I had The Ticklish Question answered only in the theoretical aspect, viz. *the child's spiritual welfare must take precedence over everything else.* But that did not answer where Kathryn should get her education.

Chefoo, the famous C.I.M. School for its missionaries' children, was in a beautiful and healthful spot by the seashore, with all kinds of recreation (land and water) available. It was staffed by missionaries whose educational qualifications were of the best. Besides, their supreme concern was the spiritual care of their pupils. The majority of the children were able to see their parents at least once a year, usually going home for a prolonged Christmas holiday. Parents in faraway pioneer places, where travel took so much time, were expected to call the children to them only once in two years. That this was lengthened more than once was usually due to the vicissitudes of war—it was not the purpose of the C.I.M. Our own girlie was separated from us for six years at one stretch because of the Japanese war, when the Japanese interned her with her school. Though they never captured us, we, of course, were not able to get to her. She was satisfied, however, that the separation was not anything that we could help.

To me the all important thing is that the child be convinced of the unwavering love of Daddy and Mummy, convinced that nobody or nothing in the work would ever compete in the parents' affections. If the little heart is convinced of this it will snuggle down and gain the sense of security a child needs.

But if the parents do not write regularly—what is the child to think? Even if the child *shows* little interest in the parents' letters (often preferring to play), the fact that the love-words have come as usual gives an unconscious satisfaction.

Also the child naturally expects that the parents will make every effort possible to see him or have him home for holidays. Parents, engrossed in their work, may not realize how their child counts on this. If the parents were *supremely concerned* about him such an opportunity, no matter how inconvenient, could hardly be neglected.

If the child is assured that the parents love him only second to the Lord Himself, then that child can take a painfully lengthened separation and not be downcast; faith will not be shaken.

So we ourselves had come to the conclusion that the C.I.M. way was the way for us. Now came the preparation of the child's heart. We did not spring it on Kathryn. When I told her that Chefoo School meant "lots and lots of children to play with" she clapped her hands in anticipation and joy. In every possible way I tried to build up a love for Chefoo before she ever went. I think this is important. Children catch "attitudes" from their parents. If the parent is secretly rebellious and critical the child will sense it and there is little possibility that the child will fit in happily, no matter how the teachers try to help him. We prayed continually that Kathy would be happy at Chefoo School, sincerely desiring what our lips asked of God. (She was!)

Since Kathryn had passed her sixth birthday while on this our first furlough, we faced putting her in Chefoo School as soon as we returned. But on the eve of our departure the war with Japan (1937) broke out and Chefoo waters were declared too dangerous for us. An alternative was to take her to Yunnan and put her in our Inter-Mission School. Her aunt, Kathryn Kuhn Harrison, lived in Kunming and our Kathy could board with her and her husband.

So we sailed from Vancouver, having to go to Japan first and then trans-ship to Hongkong. This took some weeks of course, and in the meantime, as war tensions relaxed, it was found that Butterfield & Swire ships were going safely between Hongkong and Chefoo. The Mission then decided to call Miss Grace Liddell from Yunnan temporarily to fill a place on the Chefoo staff. And as she would be trans-shipping at Hongkong the same time the Kuhn family would, it was planned that she escort Kathryn to Chefoo. So, on our arriving at Hongkong where we had expected to trans-ship to Hanoi together as a family, a telegram was handed to me before ever we disembarked. It read something like this: *"Liddell will escort Kathryn Kuhn to Chefoo from Hongkong."* And Miss Liddell herself came out in a launch to meet us and told us gently that the ship was due to leave "three days from now."

It was a severe shock to me because I was so unprepared for it. I had been making plans in my mind to put Kathy into the small school in Kunming, which would be so much nearer to us. After receiving the telegram I went down into our cabin to get Kathy ready. She was asleep in the top bunk, her pretty curly lashes dark against the soft pink cheeks. As I stood and gazed at her the thought came, "You will never again have the joy of caring for her, watching her grow and develop." I was pierced to the depths. A little box of Bible promises lay on the bed table. I seized it and cried in my heart, "Oh God, speak to me!" and drew out Ecclesiastes 11:1, "Cast thy bread upon the waters: for thou shalt find it after many days." I felt it was His voice saying, "Cast thy child upon ME. I will take good care of her and after many days thou shalt have her back again, more securely yours in heart and spirit than ever she was in mere flesh." I cannot tell you how it comforted me. I clung to it. But because I continually dwelt on what I was losing ("This is the last time I give her her bath, the last time I buckle on her sandals, the last time I comb her hair," etc.), I was in torture. Never can I forget the agony of those hours in Hongkong when we said goodbye and after the ship pulled out.

Miss Liddell was everything I could have wished and more, and long before they reached Chefoo Kathryn had learned to love her like an "own" aunt. It meant that at Chefoo, among the staff, there was one who was like a mother to her, one who was familiar and "brought familiar comforting."

As for me, John's kindness and patience is a memory for which I can never cease to bless God. For the twenty-four hours after Kathryn left and before our own ship was due to leave, he walked the streets with me. He never even seemed to weary. He just stayed with me until I was so physically exhausted I could lie down and drop into oblivion. How grateful I was and am for that patience and indulgence, only the Lord knows! I was wrong to get distraught, and the Lord Himself was going to deal with me about it. But I was quietly indulged until the time that I could bear correction. As I look back on it now, I am completely satisfied with the Lord's choosing and working.

Just before the calamity of capture by the Japanese, little daughter had a spiritual experience which prepared her to take it victoriously. Only God could have arranged that! And only He could have planned that our beloved Mrs. J. O. Fraser, with her three daughters, was interned along with Kathryn and "mothered" her during those days of scarce mail and prolonged separation from us.[1]

[1] In internment camp for long months Kathy's mail had not been delivered to her, but once free again aboard the *Gripsholm*, a Red Cross agent handed her a pack of letters from her parents. Tearing them open she made a thrilling discovery: she had a baby brother! By that time, to Kathy's amazement, Danny was already six months old! C.C.

Kathryn was repatriated on the second mercy trip of the *Gripsholm* and took notice of the preserving care of God for them on their long trip round by India and South America. The *Gripsholm* had a lighted cross at the top of the ship and it seemed to the little twelve-year-old a symbol of the presence of Christ, leading and protecting them.

Arriving in America, she was taken into the home of George and Magdalene Sutherland, of the C.I.M. Home Staff in Philadelphia. And she was cared for like a daughter until we could return from China ourselves. The Sutherlands were friends of ours since Moody days and they acted as Kathryn's foster-parents.

In the goodness of God to us after our second furlough I was with Kathryn nearly two years before leaving again for another term in China. The Japanese war had left communications and travel so disrupted that women and children were not allowed back immediately, which lengthened my normal furlough span. When we left her she was again taken into the Sutherlands' home and during the difficult high-school years she had their love and guidance to help her.

In 1950 I was back with her. The Communist turn-over had occurred, and I had taken Danny and fled out through Burma. John stayed behind to help the church. By this time Kathy was in Wheaton College, so we made for Wheaton. Again the Lord prolonged my stay with her into two years. I was a year and a half waiting for John to be released from China and then he needed a six months' rest before our arduous pioneer work in Thailand. But God had seen to it that our girlie had her mother during the last two important college years.

So "the ticklish question" of how to educate our daughter was solved step by step as it was submitted to Him. We had had long separations, but we had also had two years continual living together *twice over*.

Just before we sailed for Thailand in 1952 we saw Kathy off for the Aldrich home while she took a course in the Multnomah Bible School in Portland, Oregon.

Kathy wanted some experience of life in the business world without the shelter of a Christian home, so she accepted a teaching post at Grass Valley, Oregon. By the end of that year she knew God wanted her on the mission field. So the next time she and I met, our Kathy was an accepted candidate of the China Inland Mission. Out on the field in North Thailand she met Don Rulison, M.A. and Master of Forestry, and they became engaged and were married.

And so we all concluded "As for God, his way is perfect."

Part Three

THE VISION REALIZED

CHAPTER ONE

PEN OF A READY WRITER

ISOBEL KUHN closed the large loose-leaf binder she had been using as she wrote the preceding chapters.

"Well," she sighed, "I just can't do any more. I can't see plainly enough. I haven't the strength to go on."

She had done her final writing. It was the eighth of her now published book-length manuscripts.

And she laid down her pen.

It was an old one. For years it had worked hard for her. Miles and miles her thoughts had driven it back and forth over endless pages.

With eyes fixed on her one vision, Isobel had used her pen most purposefully. It had gleaned Bible notes and scattered them around, reaping a soul-crop by the way. It had collected inspiring quotations and sung them out to the faint-hearted, teaching, warning and encouraging them.

Friends and fellow-missionaries as well as nationals were inspired by Isobel's personal letters. "She rejoiced with those who rejoiced and wept with those who wept," commented Edna McLaren, one of the workers of the North Thailand team. "Her letters were a blessing and a challenge to the very highest, with always that rare combination of human humour and deep spirituality—never 'sermony' letters, but just a phrase, or a small quotation was left to bring its own challenge."

The "rare combination" had showed itself early in Isobel's missionary career. There it was even in her very first form-letter from China, headed Yangchow, December 24, 1928. That letter was charted so well that twenty-five years of her remarkably acceptable "circulars" plied much the same course. An immediate play for attention, some pleasantry and words of appreciation gave the letter a good start.

"Christmas Eve in China! . . . Santa Claus will need his umbrella and galoshes tonight." With this easy approach her friendship sailed through to the hearts of far-away acquaintances. She avoided *en route* all the icebergs of formal introductory sentences.

Then followed word pictures, well focused, of the work and workers around her. Some of these seemed to be taken in full sun, some in shadow. There were spots of wit and nudges of challenge, reaches for prayer help, mentions of God's goodness. Of all her subsequent writing, there was hardly a page that did not include these same elements. Besides, she always tucked in Bible promises and bits of inspiration in the form of poetry, well chosen.

Intuitively Isobel seemed to make the intimate approach to her audience that draws forth an intimate response.

Sometimes parts of her letters were as uninhibited as neighbourly chit-chat over the garden fence. That made them most acceptable. Somewhat bulky, too! She did not stop to strip them of unnecessary words. Yet the trivialities she included mixed themselves into a picture unique in realism—a candid portrait of a woman's every day life on a pioneer field. Though she wrote of grim experiences, figuratively speaking Isobel did not use sombre grey paper for her correspondence. Hers were cheerful letters with an atmosphere of contentment about them.

"Isobel is a happy writer," commented her father. "The talent she has for making an interesting letter from a small incident is really one of the gifts from the hand of God."

Actually it was he, Mr. Miller, living in Vancouver, who gave Isobel's circular letters a good launching! With his usual enthusiasm, he saw to it that what his daughter wrote to him personally was freely passed around. Beginning with family friends, the circle widened. More and more hands stretched out until even as early as 1931 he found himself issuing five hundred letters at a time. "Of course," he admitted, "a great number are local, Vancouver and district, and yet we mail many to Toronto and to other parts of the country, as well as to China."

Soon Isobel's pen work was welcomed by strangers as well as by old friends. As one of them said, "Isobel's Prayer Trust letters were always a spiritual tonic." This was the general reaction.

The mailing list kept adding weight. Then when a few years of economic depression came along Mr. Miller was overwhelmed. But what could be done? In Lisuland the Kuhns felt their increasing need for the prayer help the letters brought them. Blessing abounded in their work, but problems too scattered themselves into the rich harvest like noxious weeds. Obviously, however, busy people like John and Isobel themselves could not undertake the labour and expense of despatching hundreds of letters across oceans and continents. Even surface mail, hopelessly slow, was costly, while air rates for a quantity were unthinkable.

And another angle of the matter prodded them just then. As Isobel described that time of perplexity, "Few of those who received our circulars ever acknowledged them so we could not be sure they prayed."

So what happened?

They decided to write only to a few friends they actually knew were praying. At the same time they asked three things definitely of the Lord. Isobel enumerated them:

"1. That He would use the letters to stir up more prayer for us and the nationals.

"2. That, if more people should have a copy, to find a way somehow to multiply it.

"3. That, if it be His will, He would lay it on some heart to help with the expenses of stamps, etc. Only once in seven years had anyone ever sent money marked 'for circular-letter expense.'"

The response came and she exulted over it. "When we received Mrs. Kready's letter telling of a group of praying people who had taken us on, we were quite thrilled. And even more so when she told us that a Miss Zimmerman was multiplying the letters for us. (What a lot of tedious hours of kindness are folded up in that simple statement! God bless her for it and all who assisted.) Then a mail brought us a gift of ten dollars marked 'From the Lancaster Prayer Group.' The same mail brought a second gift from a second group lately raised up to pray, whom we have never met. Their gift was definitely marked 'for circular letter.' And three other prayer groups have arisen, whom we have never seen. In all, God has given us (of new ones), you in Lancaster, one group in Muskegon, Ill., one group in Keokuk,

Iowa, one group in Beaver, Pa., and one in Birmingham, England. We've never been given 'groups' before. Isn't God good! All three prayers answered! Truly, often we have not simply because we did not ask. 'Lord increase our faith!' "

For the first few years of their life together John and Isobel collaborated in writing the circular letters for John also wrote well. They signed together. Eventually, however, Isobel took over almost entirely.

It happened this way. Isobel knew how to tell a story to the best advantage. And when her imagination embellished it with a few flourishes, John frowned a bit, John being a stickler for accuracy.

One day Isobel was telling a story at the dining-table; "And it was pouring rain," she said.

John stopped her.

"I don't remember that it was 'pouring rain,' Belle. As I remember, it was merely raining."

"Well," she retorted, indignant at having her perfectly good story slowed down, "I didn't stop to count the raindrops."

After that when inaccuracies crept into her stories he teased her about not having stopped to count the raindrops. This fell on a resentful spot in Isobel's heart.

For some time, letter-writing day with its small arguments, became to her what she called "an exasperating trial." To count raindrops or not to count raindrops, that was the question.

"Is this word for word what each person said?" John would ask, blue pencil poised.

"My dear husband," the story-teller groaned, "I don't know shorthand. I didn't take it down verbatim. But you know yourself that was, in general, how the conversation went."

"All right," responded John, "say so. Say that this is your interpretation of the conversation."

"But that is perfectly ridiculous," Isobel protested. "Every reader knows that a conversation can't be remembered word for word."

Yet finally, the One who ties up the raindrops with a bow in the clouds untied the couple's tensions with a spirit of patience, forgiveness and mutual recognition of each other's gifts.

No more stormy letter-writing days!

Years afterwards Isobel drew from this incident some significant conclusions. "I feel many modern marriages are wrecked on just such sharp shoals as this," she said. "A human weakness is pointed out. The correction is resented. Argument grows bitter. Young people, with the novels and shows that teach false ideals of marriage, are not prepared to bear and forbear. They are not ready to forgive, not willing to endure. Divorce is too quickly seized upon as the way out. It is the worst way out! To pray God to awaken the other person, to be patient until He does so—this is God's way out. And it moulds the two opposite natures into one invincible whole."

And that is just what the Lord did for John and Isobel Kuhn. "I have thanked God for this experience," Isobel confessed, "thanked Him many times. God was preparing to use my pen in relating stories of His work in human hearts. I couldn't afford to let that pen grow careless as to facts. The blue pencil showed me that a Christian writer can't be too particular that every point be according to reality."

Eventually, John's attitude changed too. He gave her entire freedom as to what she wrote and how she wrote it. "I only helped her check certain dates and doctrines," he explained.

As they applied the love of Christ as an adhesive, the uneven edges of their temperaments were bonded into a closer union that held. It not only survived the stresses and strains. It surmounted them.

Doubtless they were temperamentally different. Perhaps they had little normal home life. But in the great essential they were absolutely one. With one heart and one mind they were united in one vision only, "Looking unto Jesus."

Some have even thought Isobel wrote the intimate "Vistas" of their testings only for the eyes of her own children. But Isobel denied this. She explained that she hoped some young couples might be helped by the spiritual secrets she and John had discovered in their married life. Certainly without God's help, most marriages never would have endured the shattering experiences she and John shared. Their twenty years on the China-Burma border with its extremely rough and unsettled living conditions, grave hazards and stretched-out separations, were desperately hard on both husband and wife!

Isobel's writing entertained her on many a day that otherwise might have been dismal and lonely. Her pen was like a companion. She once said, "If I have something to say, writing is just fun; it is housework that makes the ass long-faced and weary!" Besides, her pen was her messenger boy—always ready to run her errands. By it she kept in touch with her always-trekking husband, guarded her children and held on to her friends.

Understandably the circle of these friends kept expanding. At one time 1,700 were receiving her monthly Prayer Trust letters. One of them typically expressed what a crowd of others have said:

"I am just one among scores, perhaps hundreds, whose lives have been touched and influenced through Isobel's correspondence. I have never had the privilege of sitting down to a personal visit with her, and yet in my heart, she is one of my intimate friends. As she wrote about her humble Lisu, many a time the problems and temptations which they faced have found an echo in my own heart, and in praying for them, I was strengthened and helped in my own life.

"Perhaps because she herself was so humble, she was able to enter into their lives with such sympathy and understanding. Then, with her gifted pen and vivid imagination she was able to portray them to us. In consequence, these people of another tongue and nation, whom we don't expect ever to see on this earth, are as real to us as our neighbours down the block.

"At our house, we pray daily by name for Lisu. We have heard no news of them for the past five years and perhaps may never hear again. But Isobel made them our friends and we can't forget them."

So truly the testimony of this Vancouver friend summarized Isobel's work!

As God's liaison officer she linked the pray-ers and the prayed-for. Of course they were wide poles apart geographically and socially. Yet Christian kinship is a marvellous reality. And they experienced it. As they separately approached the one Mediator between God and man, they found themselves bound to Him and to each other.

The letters that summoned such effectual prayer help were themselves planted in prayer. For some years, in fact until

Danny's advent made it impossible, Isobel spent one morning a month in fasting and prayer. She especially asked for her own spiritual needs and those of the churches, as well as for world revival. And it was on those days, too, that she usually gathered most of her seed thoughts for her Prayer Trust letters. It took vision and self-discipline to find time and a quiet place for such exacting work. Sometimes she resorted to a favourite spot near a great pine-tree, an inspiring monarch of the forest. But the inspiration for her writing, as all will agree, came from a Source far higher than those treetops.

Certainly the hard-worked pen in Isobel Kuhn's hand was filled with something more than common ink.

Of course Isobel's love for reading greatly contributed to her success as an author. She spent little or no time with magazines. For a time she read no fiction. But later she came back to it. That was when she was sitting alone at meals in the Lisuland shanty. Then she liked to read classical fiction. Far from her own land, she found diversion in meeting her fellow-countrymen on the pages of a book propped up before her. Most systematically, however, Isobel gave her mind to devotionally stimulating books. She frequently mentioned such writers as Ruth Paxson, Oswald Chambers and Amy Carmichael of the Dohnavur Fellowship. About the latter, Isobel wrote to a friend, "Miss Carmichael could write about anything or anybody and be a blessing, her words are always so full of the Lord. . . . I read everything by her that I can get my hands on."

And this was obvious. Amy Carmichael's thoughts and poems and style appear often in Isobel's correspondence and books. In fact someone referred to her as "The C.I.M. Amy Carmichael." Similar comments being rumoured in Isobel's hearing brought out a facetious retort. She wrote to an intimate fellow-worker, "This poor earth misses dear Amy Carmichael so much that they seize her laid-down halo and try to fit it on the first Irish girl they spy. It doesn't fit!"

CHAPTER TWO

EXPERIENCES, FULL-ORBED

AND Isobel was right. A halo, no matter whose, did not fit her. She was too definitely human for that. But like Amy Carmichael, she was a good writer, and they each fitted snugly into someone's astute definition:

"The good writer is the person with full-orbed experiences and a sensitive heart and mind."

There is no denying that Isobel's experiences were "full-orbed." She shared those usual experiences of other women who are students, teachers, wives, mothers and housekeepers. But she added as well, the experiences of a missionary pioneer, a public speaker and world traveller. And she was no stranger to the experiences of suffering brought about by war, sickness and isolation. Besides, threaded through all this gamut there were significant spiritual experiences, secret dealings with God, miraculous answers to her prayers for guidance, financial provision, deliverance from dangers and besetting sins.

What experiences!

Anyone who reads a few pages of her writing soon discovers that Mrs. Kuhn was a woman with a heart and mind sensitive both to God and to humanity. Especially did her affection flow for anyone who seemed to need her help—her converts, her own children, young missionaries, young churches, the Lisu.

And in return young people responded to her. On furloughs there always followed a wave of interest in the tribes wherever the Kuhns were speaking. Isobel's own daughter Kathryn said she could listen to her mother tell the same story a dozen times and still be fascinated. One of Kathy's young friends, now a C.I.M. missionary in Laos, tells of the meetings where Mrs. Kuhn addressed the students at the Multnomah School of the Bible. The girls were so much impressed that after Isobel spoke they just quietly slipped away to pray. Of course, this sort of response was what Isobel most desired—that her message would not attract to herself, but to the Lord.

Her husband banked on her sympathetic prayer help in his ministry. "The bulwark of her prayers" as he expressed it. When he left for the first of his long trips after their marriage, he stayed a month or two visiting the Lisu tribe. Someone at that time observed Isobel. "I was at home that month and I saw Isobel was lonely. It was then she told me that she had promised the Lord that she would never stand in John's way if he felt led to go away for the gospel's sake. And she never has."

A young woman confided an intimate experience illustrating Isobel's sensitive desire to be right with the Lord not only outwardly but also inwardly. "She came to me one evening and asked to see me privately, so I invited her into my room. With tears in her eyes she asked me to forgive her. I knew nothing she had done that required my forgiveness. So she explained, saying that she had been jealous of me and that the Lord had spoken to her about it. She had confessed her sin to Him, but she felt she must ask my forgiveness, too, even though I had not known she had these feelings. I couldn't believe my ears. Jealous of me? Why, she had more gifts than I, and she was filling a useful place. But it just shows how conscientiously she was trying to follow the Lord."

Keeping her one vision in focus, she was determined that the *good* things of life must not displace the *best* things. More than one or two who lived under her roof observed how she chose to simplify home chores in order to make more time for a purely spiritual ministry: prayer, study, teaching and counselling. As Miss Nellie DeWaard recalls: "Isobel was the hostess in Tali, with a lot of guests to look after. Good servants were hard to get and Isobel never quite liked housekeeping; her talents and inclinations were quite otherwise. So the fact that she made a success of it was all the more remarkable. She created a pleasant atmosphere in the home and I am sure no guest ever went away feeling unwanted. She got a woman to help and taught her about a week's menus. It was quite easy if you lived there long enough, to know what you would have that day for dinner, but it still was varied enough that you did not get tired of it. It really was a sensible plan."

Speaking of that same time, about 1930, Isobel once remarked to Mr. Harry Owen that all the other young workers in the mission station were able to give undivided attention to study, while she had to spend much time in housekeeping. As this slowed her progress in language study, she was tempted to feel resentful. But, recognizing the danger, she resolved to spend an hour a night in Bible study. This enabled her to triumph over the sin of resentment and discontent; as she herself testified, "No one could spend an hour a day studying the Bible without something happening in the spiritual area."

Mr. Charles Peterson had fifteen years to observe Isobel at first hand in Lisuland where he shared mission station life with her and John at Oak Flat. His cabin sat on the slope just below the "House of Grace" as the Kuhns called their home. It was really he who was in charge of the station and a right arm of assistance to Isobel during John's long absences on Mission business.

Charles remembers a story of life at Oak Flat during the days of World War II. "We had been carrying on a full programme of village work and Bible Schools on the east bank of the Salween River. The Japanese were on the west bank. During the day we could often hear the boom of the Japanese guns. In the evening we sometimes saw fires from villages which they had lighted. We had planned that just as soon as the news came that they had crossed the river we would leave and make our way through the mountains into the Mekong River country. Then one night—well, I was sound asleep in my log cabin when one of the Lisu fellows rapped on the door.

" 'Teacher,' he said, 'the Japanese are coming. Ma-ma says that you are to come up to the House of Grace.' When I got there Isobel told me that Luke had been up to one of the high villages and had heard fighting at the river crossing. (Deduction: the Japanese are coming.)

'Isobel suggested we read a psalm. I began to read the 91st Psalm which would have been my reading when morning came. When I came to the words, 'Thou shalt not be afraid of . . . the terror by night,'

" 'That's enough, Charlie,' she said, 'Good night.'

"Outside the whole village was in turmoil. Barking dogs,

squealing pigs, crying children, shouting parents. But Isobel had heard God's voice and had gone to sleep.

"In the morning we learned what had happened. Someone from the east bank of the river had stolen the ferryboat and was rowing towards the west bank. Natural result—gun fire, an excited Lisu, and a woman's bravery which I shall never forget."

Quite literally Isobel took God at His word. Though her imaginative nature easily conjured up all sorts of alarms, yet her confidence was in the Lord. And He developed in her the highest kind of courage, a boldness to push on straight through frightening situations despite her fears.

Victorious experiences!

For instance, she was timid about riding over the mountains. Often she tried to walk when in dangerous places. But sometimes she was too tired. So she was forced to ride. Lucius, a fine Lisu lad, usually accompanied her, leading the mule. One day, however, when for the moment he was not at its head, the road turned suddenly and rose sharply over a bank. The mule lost his foothold. With a drop of hundreds of feet over the edge of the narrow path, Isobel felt herself still mounted—but over space.

"Oh God! Oh God!" she cried.

Stamping hoofs beat the air, stumbled, clambered and clung finally to terra firma. Isobel was unnerved and limp.

But she kept on riding.

"By nature I dislike travel and change," Isobel admitted. Yet she adjusted herself to the packing and juggling of suitcases, the endless changing from place to place, and people to people.

By ship, by rail, by plane and bus, by sedan and mountain chair, by mule and by foot, she covered the miles. She circled the world more than twice as she burrowed deep into the depths of Asia. Repeatedly on furlough she sped across the North American continent. These were the longer spans of travel. But within these spheres her downsittings and uprisings were considerable. During the time she and John were first assigned to Chinese work, Isobel said she thought that she had visited every town and city in that whole populous area. Afterwards, as they worked in Lisuland, travel was still more rough and dangerous. But since she was on service for the King of kings, *she kept on travelling*.

Once an aching tooth prodded her into making an excursion

to the dentist. It was no pleasure trip. As Isobel came winding down the mountain trails on her mule, she was dreading the long stretch of Burma Road that loomed ahead of her. Her fear was quite understandable. Without regular bus service, travellers just chanced catching a ride on a Chinese cargo truck, piling on top of boxes, bundles and bales. Perched there they held on for dear life. Usually while on dizzy down-grades, the driver turned off the ignition and coasted. Wrecks pitched over the road's edge added nothing to the scenery nor to passengers' sense of security!

Thinking of these things, Isobel shuddered as she approached the Big Road. There to her great relief, however, she discovered a couple of General Chenault's "Flying Tigers," American air-men, driving through to Kunming. Off she started with them for an eventful four days' journey.

"We were to leave at half-past five in the morning," Isobel recalled. "I arose about four o'clock in order to have a quiet time with the Lord first. I had been up early on the trail so many mornings, and travelling till dark, that I debated whether or not to skip my time of worship that day and get a little more sleep. But the habit of *God first* formed in Moody days, stood me in good stead now. For God had something particular to say to me. Yet when I lit my lamp at that early hour and turned my sleepy eyes on the portion for the day (Genesis 28) I had the feeling, 'Oh, just the story of Jacob's ladder.' Is it the lazy flesh or the devil that puts such thoughts into our heads? I turned my sluggishness over to the Lord in prayer first, and then as I read that old story so familiar from childhood, verse 15 sprang out of the page as if I had never read it before.

"'*And behold I am with thee, and will keep thee in all places whither thou goest.*' The Lord's voice came clear and unmistak-able: 'This is My promise to you for the journey ahead.'"

How thankful she was on many occasions for such an assur-ance! For one night along the way where they stayed at a hostel, a drunken man attempted to bash in her door in the dead of night! Then also, on the last day of their trip the car broke down completely. Besides, while it stood awaiting repairs it was thoroughly looted, Isobel's belongings included.

But Isobel finally reached the dentist and got the relief she needed. She had spent eight and a half days of travel to get it!

Somewhere on her journey, she was alarmed by the news that Rangoon (Burma) had fallen to the Japanese. And now in Kunming, that large provincial capital, dreadful war rumours dinned in her ears. Behind her a stampeding herd of pitiable refugees quickly filled the Burma Road. Back in that tumult of bombing and carnage John was doing what he could to rescue any stranded missionaries. Isobel had no way of communicating with him.

Fightings without and fears within left the lone wife a feeling of acute desolation. She seized an opportunity to escape to the province of Szechwan. There "she was lost without her Lisu," said her hostess, Mrs. Arnold Lea. Isobel was also most distraught because she felt she had run off to Szechwan in panic rather than at the Lord's bidding.

Finally, as she and her pretty Chinese girl companion, Eva Tseng, started back to Kunming they had a hairbreadth escape from a vicious native driver in whose truck they were riding. A terrifying experience. Yet repeatedly they were aware of God keeping His promise, "I am with thee and will keep thee in *all* places whither thou goest."

"I had been tossed from pillar to post for six weary months," Isobel sighed. "I could hardly wait to get home to my quiet bedroom by the side of the deep ravine where the birds sang matins, and the great peaks glowed back the sunset hues with their steady unshakeableness at day's end. I longed to get my roots down." But in Kunming Isobel learned that her brother-in-law, Dave Harrison, must make a trip to some needy churches in the country. Would she consider teaching his Bible class of Chinese university students in order to free him for that itineration?

"I did not want to stay in Kunming. I wanted to get to John as soon as possible. I was desperately longing for him to put his arms around me and comfort me. But," she explained, "where common sense clearly points out a duty, that is the voice of God. We do not need any other, provided a higher duty is not claiming us." So she stayed on, having consented to teach. No wonder she could add, "The students' class began to grow. One day I was asked if I would teach a second Bible class, a morning class for Christians. Soon I was teaching three classes, and one young man had accepted Christ as Saviour."

And that was recompense enough for Isobel for all the frustrations of the road that lay behind her and for the sacrifice of her desire to see John's face.

Sensitively, Isobel's heart and mind responded to the Lord's discipline. She permitted her full-orbed experiences to press her closer to Christ. Then the bitter experiences became rewarding ones: her life was deepened and her service enriched. The Lord was teaching His pupil the joyful ultimate of all experiences, intimacy with Himself.

CHAPTER THREE

PRESSING ON

"LORD, we are just three zeros, but Thou art our Leader, and that makes 1,000." Informally, Isobel spoke her mind to the Lord. And her words stood out bold-typed in Charles Peterson's memory. The three missionaries were kneeling together in the shanty: Isobel, John and Charles. It was on a Saturday afternoon, preceding the Monday opening of the very first Rainy Season Bible School.

There had been short Bible schools from almost the beginning of missionary work in Lisuland. But the Rainy Season Bible School was quite different. It was timed to fill profitably the three months when farming made the least demands on the tribesfolk.

It was Isobel's own idea.

At first the Lisu church leaders were sceptical about the plan. But "Ma-ma" persuaded them to give it a trial. Meanwhile she consulted with Mr. J. O. Fraser, then the C.I.M. Provincial Superintendent. He heartily approved.

But Fraser never lived to see the great success of the new project, for about that time he contracted a virulent type of malaria. His Home-call left the irreparable vacancy in the work that in due time brought John Kuhn into the office of Superintendent for West Yunnan. From that time the Chinese churches and missionaries on the plain claimed much of John's energy. So Isobel went on with preparations for the proposed Rainy Season Bible School. She planned carefully and prayed earnestly. She herself taught as well as enlisted the help of others. She prepared her lessons in outline well ahead of time, then when the sessions began she chalked them on the blackboard and required her classes to memorize them.

Once Isobel declared, "I love to teach the Bible. Evangelism was never my gift, but the opening of the Scriptures feeds and blesses the teacher even more than it does the student."

Actually, she did not have any Lisu text of the Bible to teach!

(Only a few books of it were then in writing. Even during those very years Allyn and Leila Cooke, with the assistance of Mr. Fraser and the Lisu evangelist Moses Fish, were throwing themselves into the translation of the Lisu New Testament.)[1]

It did not baffle Ma-ma, however, that she had so few books of the Bible to use—it simply was more of a challenge to her as a student and as a teacher. And when the first session of the Bible School was concluded, it had proved so successful that Isobel reported jubilantly, "A most blessed time, thrilling proof that this was what the Lisu church needed!"

That was in 1938.[2]

Ever after that the R.S.B.S. continued. Probably Isobel Kuhn's greatest contribution as a missionary for twenty years in China was through the Rainy Season Bible School. In addition to the regular session, the first special school for young women was started in 1942. In 1943 the first special school for young men began, and in 1943 and 1944 there followed the first special sessions for children.

Year by year bare feet came filing along the mountain trails converging on Oak Flat village. But also, year after year, problems piled up, threatening to block the whole programme. At one time paratyphoid broke out among the staff. Just before another session, Charles came down with rheumatic fever. Then one year infant Danny, doubled up with colic, kept his mother heavy-eyed because of disturbed nights. Before another session, shortness both of staff and supplies made the prospect of a school seem hopeless. Most serious of all, however, was the fact that during some of those years the missionaries were separated only by a few mountain ridges from one of the hottest contests of a global war.

"The Japanese were just across the mountains from us. We were never allowed to forget them," Isobel declared. Soldiers appeared at most unexpected times and places. Since the local tribespeople had never seen a Japanese, they suspected every strange uniform and panicked easily.

---

[1] It was finally published in 1951.

[2] The same year Isobel Kuhn's first little book was published, i.e. *Precious Things of the Lasting Hills* (out of print).

"Those days," Isobel commented, "the whole world was learning from England what a boost to a nation's morale is the spirit of 'Blitz or no blitz, we carry on business as usual.' "

"Business as usual? Impossible for Oak Flat! . . . but—well, let's stick to it as long as we can, and see what God does for us." This wavering between faith and foreboding was a periodic temptation. But when they decided to ignore peril and go steadily on with their usual programme, their fortitude had a wonderfully stabilizing effect on the whole countryside.

Hundreds gathered for the 1942 Christmas festival.

Yet among that crowd, when Isobel asked how many young women planned to come to the Girls' Bible School in February, not one would promise. The Lisu work was wholly indigenous, so of course all students would take care of their own expenses. But money was always scarce. Local taxes were high. War rumours were unsettling. Understandably, the young women asked: "What if we came and then the military situation turned bad suddenly? We couldn't get back across the river to our homes!"

That was a real objection.

"But as 1943 dawned," Isobel commented, "all seemed quiet. Then came the problem. Should we prepare for a Girls' School without the promise of even one scholar? Charles and I prayed about it and decided to go on as if life were normal. If the Lord didn't say 'Stop!' wasn't it common sense to infer that He meant 'Go ahead!'? So we decided to have the dormitories repaired."

As Charles just then was to be out of the village, holding other Bible classes, it was up to Ma-ma to hire the workmen and oversee the job. At that particular time John was far off, attempting to rescue Mr. and Mrs. Fred Hatton, who were still within Japanese-controlled territory at Stockade Hill. Consequently Charles and Isobel knew they must conduct the School without John's help. Eva Tseng was on hand, however. She was an educated Chinese girl, an earnest Christian, and almost as devoted to Isobel as a daughter. Capable and willing, she assumed responsibility in house work and did some teaching as well.

Isobel had good reason to remember that session of the R.S.B.S.

"As the day for assembling at Girls' Bible School drew near, the weather turned against us. Snow clouds came down over the great peaks (12,000 to 15,000 feet high), the wind blew icy cold, and on the lower slopes the snow turned to rain—penetrating, chill, damp. The girls on the west bank of the Salween would have more than twenty miles of mountain road to travel, besides crossing a dangerous river—which they would not dare attempt in a snowstorm.

"Saturday was assembling day and by night fall we had over a dozen girls, but all from the east bank. Now our most progressive students (mentally and spiritually) were those who lived on the west bank, so you can imagine how we prayed for them to come.

"Sunday continued stormy. But Monday there was a lull. The sky was dull and grey all day, but at least there was no downpour. We began the school with the girls we had.

"You can imagine our thrill at sunset when a shout came ringing up the trail, 'Girls from the west bank are coming.'

"We ran to the door, and there around the edge of the mountain was a line of little dots moving down the trail towards us! We stepped out gingerly, for the ground was too wet and slippery to allow speed. There they were—their bedding and books in big bags slung over their shoulders or carried on the back with the strap placed over the forehead to distribute the weight. Mary, Lydia, Julia, Chloe—and their brothers or husbands coming on behind, carrying their grain supply! Happy smiles and handshakes. 'We were afraid you wouldn't make it,' was answered by a chorus of girlish exclamations as to the difficulties encountered and their determination to press through. Chatter, chatter, as bare feet pattered over the muddy trails to the church kitchen where warm fires and a hot supper were waiting.

"That night, for the first evening session of the school, we had thirty-three students! And what a praise service! How it pays to take one step at a time with God! What if we had not prepared the dormitories? That very night the storm descended again and kept it up for a week. Sometimes His door opens only for a very short period, and if one is not fully ready to enter in, it will close, perhaps permanently. With so many bright-faced girls to teach, Charles, Eva and I swung into the school work with joy and zest."

So the girls' session that began in bad weather came to a sunny ending. And this cut itself into a pattern; first came troubles, tangling plans, then the Lord's hand moved, setting things in order. Obstacles always gave way as Ma-ma and the staff pressed on, believing in the God of the impossible to change things and people.

"Find out what God wants you to do," said Isobel, "and deliberately put aside 'wind-words' (alarming rumours) and press on with your job."

The Lisu caught the spirit, and the R.S.B.S. prospered even when Ma-ma and Ma-pa were absent on furlough.

CHAPTER FOUR

ALWAYS A MISSIONARY

IT was in October, 1944 the Kuhns flew over the Hump to India. World War II was still in full swing. Incidentally it was then they discovered that the famous Hump route hovered right over their own section of Lisuland. From India a troopship transported them as refugees over the Indian and Pacific oceans, finally landing them safely in Southern California after thirty-six difficult days aboard. With little delay they hurried off to Philadelphia. There daughter Kathryn joined them. She had been under the wing of Mr. and Mrs. George Sutherland while attending high-school. For the first time they were united as a family of four—and incidentally that was Kathryn's first introduction to her little brother.

Whether in Lisuland or America, wherever Isobel went, she was always a missionary, an effective and tactful one too, on ships, on buses, on the platform, in her home. Like an angler, she was keen to make a cast in the stream of life, hoping for a strike. To audiences of cultured people or groups of tribal folk she kept pressing on with the message of salvation through the Lord Jesus.

Behind this eagerness and explaining it in part, there was a story Isobel liked to tell against herself. Away back in Moody Institute days, the students had been listening to an inspiring address on soul winning, the speaker stressing the duty of speaking to someone each day. Isobel was stirred and decided that before leaving the building she would speak to someone about the Lord. Sitting at the end of the row, she waited and scanned faces nearby. Finally she asked a lady, "Are you saved?" The lady eyed her and said, "Are you one of the young missionary candidates?" "Yes," said Isobel eagerly. "Then," said the lady, "just pray the Lord to give you tact!"

Perhaps it was because Isobel heeded both the admonition of the speaker as well as the rebuke of the lady that she became so sympathetically responsive to people in need of spiritual help. If her tongue spoke out too quickly or too freely at times, at least it was not tied in knots of silence when she saw a chance to speak a good word for the Saviour.

1945 found the John Kuhn family in Dallas, Texas, in a home of their own, while John studied in Dallas Theological Seminary. "In a short time," Isobel recalled, "we were having a small group come to our home every Friday night for Bible study and prayer. As I look back now, every single couple of that group reached the foreign field. Italy, Switzerland, Formosa, China, the border of Nepal and the border of Afghanistan, have felt the touch of Christ through those lives."

Isobel enjoyed those days of being a good neighbour, a mother and a "keeper at home." Yet she was aware of her one vision; she did not forget that, after all, she was essentially a missionary and that the Lisu were her special responsibility. She wrote to her tribal friends, prayed for them, and enlisted others to help in prayer. She wrote about them, too, finishing her second book, Nests Above the Abyss.[1]

A good friend of Isobel after reading the book with understanding expressed her reaction:

> "God, look upon them tenderly
>   The little homes that lie
> Up high upon the ridges
>   Beneath the bending sky.
>
> God, thrust abroad the messengers
>   To reach the farthest nest
> That lost ones may be gathered in
>   And numbered with the blest."
>   Dean I. MacLeod.

Then when the atom bomb changed many plans, John was called to return to China for an important tribal survey. Once again the couple were challenged by the motto of their married life, God first, as Mr. Kuhn sailed for China alone.

Husband and wife had no arguments with God about another separation.

[1] Nests Above the Abyss, C.I.M., 1947.

"The Lord gave us 2 Corinthians 4:12—'So then death work-eth in us, but life in you.' We felt the separation meant 'death' in the sense of breaking up our family life, but that the Lisu might gain spiritually."

Returning to Lisuland with Danny in 1947 Isobel had plenty of opportunity for further sacrifices. For several months of that year she was the only white missionary in that isolated part of Lisuland. That year John's demanding duties had hardly taken him from home before she had to wrestle with sickness. Danny came down with dread typhus fever. Lisu church leaders brought their most difficult church problems to her.

Spiritual conflict and physical danger lurked all along Ma-ma's path.

"From the way she has written about the Lisu believers," Mr. Ivan Allbutt[1] commented, "one feels the throb of a missionary pulse akin to that of Paul, who wrote to his converts in Galatia, 'My little children, of whom I travail in birth again until Christ be formed in you.'"

But when the tribesmen became Christians, they became Ma-ma's bodyguard vigilantly keeping watch over her when she was alone, her defender when thieves and base men were skulk-ing about at night.

In 1948 the village of Oak Flat was invaded by a band of Communist brigands. They were led by a Chinese named Dai Yi-gwan, "A man who was my personal enemy," said Ma-ma. "I had found him out in oppressing the poor Lisu and I had stood up for the people. He hated me from that day on. He was like a demon incarnate. I shudder to think what would have been my fate if God had not uprooted me and sent me across the Salween River just out of his reach."

When the missionaries moved, the Rainy Season Bible School also moved. In fact, Lucius, who had been Ma-ma's faithful Lisu assistant for years, not only supervised their removal to the Village of Olives, but built them a new house near his own. And Lisu friends, one hundred and fifty of them, lugged piles of logs from the forests to construct their house. They did not halt in their gift of labour till they also had made permanent plans for

[1] C.I.M. Publication Secretary for North America.

the R.S.B.S. They constructed dormitories to accommodate one hundred persons. Isobel said, "Laughter and perspiration were mingled in good measure and as I sat watching them I prayed in my heart that we might be worthy of their labours of love. Lucius had told me of one poor family who between them must have given almost forty days of free work on our house." And they let their own buckwheat crop wait while they gave this labour for the Lord's sake.

Such love more than compensated for Ma-ma's hardships. She met her rewards every day—smiling ones on their sandalled feet! They kept filing by her shanty door—Lisu she had mothered, "walking in the faith." As she reviewed them she agreed with the Apostle Paul when he declared that his children in the faith were his glory and joy.

"I'll never forget the inspiration it was being with those Lisu Christians, and seeing their love and devotion, not only to the Lord, but also to their missionaries." Such was Mrs. Estella Kirkman's testimony after living at the Village of Olives. She had gone there in 1948 to teach Child Evangelism in the R.S.B.S. "Every afternoon the students would get out and play volley ball, and how Isobel enjoyed watching them! She cheered and entered thoroughly into their fun." And at other times she entered as sympathetically into their trials.

Isobel balanced her rewarding experiences against those of some people she formerly observed in America. How she pitied that couple! They were childless and alone, daily going out to work just to maintain their richly ordered home. Living for their possessions. "I had a desolating sense of barrenness sweep over me," said Isobel, "and I felt the contrast and aching tragedy of those two lives, with all their God-given possibilities spent on *things*. What a terrible waste!" she exclaimed. "Oh, that we would awaken to the real values of life! And then I thought of my life. I thought of the flocks of dear warm-hearted people that run to meet us, that shout with joy at the sight of 'their missionaries,' that cry 'Thank you!' with shining eyes of gratitude after a message that has fed their hearts, that pray for us every day— lives that are beautiful in their unconscious selflessness, made so by the power of His cross."

She thrilled with the new life apparent in those who once had been dismally heathen. She felt elated with the joy of the illiterates as they learned to read. She sighed with relief when suffering bodies were cleaned up and healed, characters and homes transformed. She exulted over shy young Christians as they budded into bright teachers and blossomed into self-sacrificing evangelists. To her it was pure joy to know that by them the amazing story of Christ's death for every sinner was being sung and preached and demonstrated, far and wide.

Isobel's imagination could go climbing over the mountains and hear tribal voices echoing what they had heard in the R.S.B.S. Some from even as far as Burma and Nepal had heard the good news from her lips at those classes.

She once wrote to friends who prayed for her and her work, "How I will rejoice in heaven when I see some of *you* get your rewards! We missionaries get so many on earth here that I wonder if there will be much left to get up yonder!"

Years before, when Isobel was still at college, she had dreamed of being a college dean of girls. But as a foreign missionary, her desire to inspire and help others was not only fulfilled, but rewarded in excess of anything she had ever dreamed.

Seriously Isobel had accepted the challenge of a greater missionary teacher when he said, "The things that thou hast heard of me . . . the same *commit thou to faithful men* who shall be able to teach others also" (2 Timothy 2:2). One of Isobel's "faithful men" was named "Second Thomas." With her characteristic friendliness she had kept in touch with him while she was on furlough in 1945. His response she well might have regarded as ample reward for the life-blood she invested in China's tribesland.

"Oak Flat, October 8, 1945

"Big Sister in America,

"Because of fellowship with my beloved Jesus Christ, I, Second Thomas, the slave of Jesus Christ, send greetings to the spiritual mother who has helped my soul and whom I cannot forget but wish to reach by paper.

"Eh-eh Ma-ma, I got the letter you wrote me and the family photo. It was a great joy to me and a heart comfort. I am thanking you. I cannot reach you with my voice but I wish I could have fellowship with you.

"Eh-eh, it was God's pleasure that I was at Oak Flat those four years. I know it. Ma-ma if it had not been for your teaching and exhorting and for God's keeping, I would have forgotten God and been a wicked fellow, I know it. But God in the fullness of His pity saved me. But here I came to teach, and I studied, and read and woke up and was careful and kept myself" (he quotes the words of Jude 21). "I thank God very very much.

"In April I had a great sorrow because of this old nature of mine. I was heartbroken with grief. I know it was because I lost my temper. I confessed in front of everybody that it was not God's will. I've been ashamed many times. Please pray for me.

"The writer is the son your spirit bore.

"Second Thomas."

CHAPTER FIVE

OVER THE BACK WALL

FINALLY the day came when Isobel felt she must say good-bye to her beloved Lisu people.

Wild alarms were filling the air.

During her whole life in China she had experienced repeated political upheavals. She knew the war-pattern all too well. Fresh in her mind was her husband's 1949 experience (mentioned in the Prologue of this book). So as rough Red hands began snatching cities and villages just at the base of her mountains, Isobel's imagination ran riot. Would this mean imprisonment of foreign missionaries? Internment? Or worse?

Widespread confusion stirred up local desperadoes. Robbers, brigands and foot-loose soldiers were clambering up the crags and canyons around her.

Beside all this Isobel was concerned for Danny. At six years of age, he was beginning to understand the filthy speech he heard in the village where two-thirds of the people were still heathen. It was the boy's danger that was a deciding factor.

Isobel's mind was made up. But some years before she had run away trigger-quick when she saw war rushing towards her. From that unhappy experience she had learned her lesson. Now she waited and prayed for God's unmistakable guidance.

Isobel's courage of those days was clearly recalled by her co-worker, Charles Peterson: "John was absent again. It was just before the Communists came. We were holding a Bible school. One of the Lisu Christians from the northern field had been deceived by the Communists: he felt they were the saviours of the country and he expounded their principles. Then he began to send us messages as to when the Reds were coming. Finally, one morning he came into our dining-room.

" 'This is the day! Today this village will be liberated. But you have nothing to fear.'

"Even when he was speaking bullets began to hum and the

battle was on. Lucius dashed in. 'You can't stay in this bamboo house. Get into the mud house and shut the door!' We obeyed. By afternoon the Nationalists had chased the Communists out of the village, and one of the Nationalist officers pounded on the door and demanded that we come out. They questioned me. Then pointing the gun at Isobel they said, 'You've got rebels (Reds) in this house. Bring them out.'

"With entirely level tones Isobel replied, 'You are at perfect liberty to search the house, sir.'

"Of course the search revealed no rebels. And just to end the story—the room we had occupied during the day was taken over by the Nationalists that night. I slept above that room. At midnight a runner came in with the news. 'Governor Lung has capitulated. We are not to fight any longer.' And the gun-toting sergeant of the afternoon said, 'That's settled. We're all Communists now.'"

Of course the situation was anything but settled. The erupting volcano was too near for that!

Christmas Day, 1949, the Nationalist general Dwan and his soldiers withdrew, but with Reds approaching and violent men all around her, Isobel felt herself in a whirlpool of what she referred to as "real danger, horrible danger."

Remarkably protected, however, under the shadow of the Almighty, the work of the church went on. And Isobel postponed her departure. She was still awaiting indications that it was God's will for her to leave. Then to her great relief, her husband came home to the village. And he called the Lisu in for another Rainy Season Bible School. A hundred students gathered.

"The best school ever!" declared Ma-ma.

Her next step was not simple to determine. "God expects us to exercise spiritual discernment," Isobel observed, "and He guides by a certain pressure on the spirit, by a still small voice, by a something so delicately intangible that unless carefully tuned in to His Spirit, you can miss it widely. When it is only a still small voice which is our guide, it is easy for Satan to throw us into confusion by causing us to question if we have heard aright. It is a good plan not to go back on past guidance."

Then, believing the Lord was leading her, on March 10, 1950,

Isobel and Danny started away, over the western wall of China's border mountains into Burma.

The parting with John was one of the hardest they had ever had. "I felt," said Isobel, "that I wouldn't get back; that Communists would never allow evangelical Christianity to work under their régime. John is an optimist by nature, but when it came to saying goodbye, for once he could not force a smile. Danny and I left him on a high rock jutting out from the road, biting his lips to restrain his emotion. And we set our faces towards a trek that must take us half-way around the world."

First, a Lisu escort hazarded life and limb with their beloved Ma-ma and her boy, through snowy mountain passes, wild jungles, bombed bridges, to Burma. Then came gruff immigration officials with their endless red tape, and soldiers and tension everywhere. Using Chinese money, Burmese money, Siamese (Thai) money, Hongkong money, annoyed Isobel into exclaiming, "Oh! let's never mention the word again!" But, she added significantly, speaking of the whole journey, "The Lord had supplied as each need arose, but each time in a different way. Stranded at world's end? Maybe. Yet if we but lean back we will find ourselves on the bosom of Christ—sweet familiar place," and she quoted,

> "Sometimes on the Rock I tremble
> Faint of heart and weak of knee,
> But the steadfast Rock of Ages
> Never trembles under me!"

At last when on 2nd May her ship steamed into Vancouver harbour, friends she had known since girlhood opened their arms to her. There were the Elden Whipples, the Stanley Norths, the Girls' Corner Club friends as well as her own brother Murray. But she hastened on across the States to Wheaton, Illinois, for Kathryn was there, about to finish a term at the College. There Isobel poignantly felt the security of what she described as "a beautiful little college town in the heart of America! Long streets tree-shaded, with squirrels scampering happily from branch to branch. No air-raid alarms. No windows iron-barred against thieves. Just peace and plenty, the beauty of spring and gay young voices. Family life, friendships, freedom. It was like heaven on earth!"

Meanwhile John stayed firmly on in Yunnan, choosing rather to suffer awhile with the other C.I.M. missionaries for whose safety he felt responsible, than to take the less perilous escape directly from Lisuland to Burma. That hard choice detained him nearly a year, as the general evacuation of these missionaries was not authorized by the C.I.M. until December 1950.

Awaiting her husband's return, Isobel found a house in Wheaton.

In a letter she gives the whole story under the title, "Behind America's Plush Curtain." She writes:

"Thank you for praying about a place for us; we move today! And the story must begin far back, many years ago indeed, at Moody Bible Institute in 1925. Among the hundreds of students there that year, there were three girls who wanted to go to China for the gospel's sake. They were Jenny Kingston, Ella Dieken and Isobel Miller. And there were three boys who also felt called to China in that student group. They were Francis Fitzwilliam, Jack Graham and John Kuhn. And the three boys liked the three girls. In fact Fitz and John had bought an ancient Ford model-T to help them get to country places to preach, and they named it hopefully, The Jenny-Belle!

"All six went to China with the China Inland Mission. And all of them were designated to tribes work in Yunnan province. And all of them were married in China; John and Isobel were even best man and bridesmaid at Jack and Ella's wedding!

"A quarter of a century has rolled by, and by the strange workings of God the three girls find themselves together once more in Wheaton—the home town of none of them. The three girls are without the three boys. For Fitz lies buried in the Stockade Hill district, where he died of typhus while attempting to open the Kachin tribe to the gospel. And Jack died on their last furlough home. And John is still behind the Iron Curtain.

"The three girls need a home, and there is a three-apartment house at 123 Scott Street."

So the three of them decided to team up in purchasing the three-storey house. There was a separate apartment on each floor. In Isobel's four rooms on the second floor she made a

comfortable home for Kathy and Danny. There she wrote
another short book, *Stones of Fire*.[1] Besides, she took frequent
speaking engagements, taught a Bible class of college girls, and
entertained her own and her children's friends.

"Everything was so artistically chosen and arranged," recalls
a neighbour, as she lets us see things as she saw them in Isobel's
apartment. "It was quite humble, but so shining with decency
and order! Every detail; the careful hanging up of the hard-
worked broom, the tidiness of her clothes-closet, the immacu-
late condition of the bathroom, the friendly arrangement of her
few books (the Kuhns had lost their books in West China), the
bits of boy nonsense for Danny, and the white scrim Priscilla
curtains with their dainty blue ribbon lacing. Well, it was
apparent that the Lord was there and in charge of that home
always.

"I remembered that Isobel had said long ago, 'One of my
favourite quotations is "The Spirit-filled life is a daily grind!"'"

"One day she phoned me in distress. The washing machine
in the basement had stopped suddenly and would not start.
Could I tell her what was wrong? I ran across immediately, but
realized that the difficulty was not due to her missionary ignorance
of modern electrical appliances. It would not work for me,
either. We just asked God to set it going, for neither of us had
time to waste. One of us touched something—we never did find
out what. And it went. After that we often pooled our family
washings and worked together in the basement and hung things
out together in her pleasant back garden. What times of rich
fellowship!"

And to quote Isobel herself on her home in Wheaton: "As I
go about my pretty little apartment, enjoying its light and har-
mony of colour, I whisper, 'Thank Thee, Lord; but don't let my
heart get tied to it. Help me to remember it is just a tent, with
the friendship of God and of my friends upon it.' If we send our
roots down deep into a thing of earth, that very thing may set
up spiritual decay in our being."

The mother and children chose early evening, about Danny's
bedtime, for their family prayer time. Prayers over, there were

[1] *Stones of Fire*, C.I.M., 1951.

kisses in a triangular embrace accompanied by strong young hugs. One evening Dan remarked that only one thing was lacking. When questioned as to what he meant, he simply said, "Whiskers!"

One day in July, the mailman tossed in the long-desired letter, news of John's safe arrival in Hongkong—news as welcome to his wife and family as a burst of sunshine after a long foggy day. But he was to be further delayed. First, he had been appointed to make a tribal survey in North Thailand (Siam). Then in November of 1951 he was to attend an important conference held at Bournemouth in England, (C.I.M. officers and leaders there made the momentous decisions that resulted in transplanting the field personnel from China to Southeast Asia and Japan under the new name of the Overseas Missionary Fellowship of the China Inland Mission. This was probably the most crucial point in the whole eighty-six years of C.I.M. history.)

Isobel, with her heart at rest about her husband's safety, awaited his reports eagerly. He described to her North Thailand as he saw it, filled with tribes people similar to those in China, Burma and Indo-China. Utterly unreached were some 5,000 of the Lisu tribe.

"Moreover, Belle," wrote John, "we can use the Chinese language in reaching almost all of the Thailand tribes. I always found someone who understood me. And Orville Carlson and I were even able to point some souls to the Lord in the short time I was there. The government is friendly. The tribes are approachable. The field is before us. The time may be short. Missionaries have been in Thailand over a hundred years and yet have not been able to reach beyond the Thai people to the aborigines of the mountains. If we don't pioneer, they may never be reached." John's strong words challenged his wife.

Finally they were reunited and could discuss things face to face.

"But John," she protested, "we are old. It's a young man's job! And we would have to leave the children again."

At fifty years of age, must she go pioneering again, climb up rough trails, learn another tongue? Already she had worked on the Chinese and the Lisu languages. Now must she study Thai, too?

As she allowed her mind to tangle up in the foreseeable difficulties, she confessed, "Of course my heart fainted. But once I stopped contemplating the disagreeable things that might happen and turned single-eyed to the Lord, He counselled me: 'Of course there will be hard places. What of it? To choose ease rather than effort is to choose slow decay. Do you think your children would benefit by being with parents who made such a choice? You and John are needed out there. You two can hold the fort while younger people are studying languages. They may have faith, courage and strong bodies, but they do not have experience.'"

Isobel had arrived at the right conclusion. She and John were needed. Hundreds of mature workers of the C.I.M. had been roughly thrust from China by the Communists. After that ordeal, many were like disabled war veterans: they could never again face foreign service. But others, in an unbelievably short time, rallied again. And besides, pouring in were numbers of new volunteers, full of fresh vigour and spiritual vision. All were purposing to reach the unevangelized peoples in countries adjacent to China; including millions of Chinese. As Isobel foresaw, obviously the direction and counsel of seasoned missionaries were indispensable.

For instance, in Lisuland, John and Isobel Kuhn had proved the success of St. Paul's method of establishing a wholly indigenous work. Their superintendent, J. O. Fraser himself, had steadily held to this method from the time he began to evangelize the Lisu. Living sacrificially, giving the gospel persistently, he set the example for all the missionaries under his supervision, insisting that they refrain from using *any* money from abroad to hire evangelists, build chapels or subsidize students. It was the hard way of doing things as the missionaries well knew. But they could testify that when trouble struck China, the Lisu churches were standing on the firm foundation of the Rock rather than on the shifting sand of money stipends from foreign sources. In some other parts of China, only too easily were doles demonstrated to be a curse, not a blessing to the national churches.

So after evacuation from Communist China and with a new start to be made, the entire Overseas Missionary Fellowship of the C.I.M. was committed to pursue a wholly indigenous policy.

Frankly Isobel summarized the way the Lord had changed her thinking until she too was ready to launch out again.

"In March 1950, when our little son and I made our way over the high Pien Ma Pass into Burma, and then home, I felt as if I had no more courage to face the foreign field another time. The dangers, the high tension of threatened 'liberation' for more than a year, the ambush and gunfire when it actually occurred, the physical privations of the journey to safety, and the ordeal of travelling through countries where we did not speak the languages, had seemed the limit a human being could take.

" 'I will soon be middle-aged now,' I told myself. 'I'm too old for such arduous living any more. I'd like to get work and stay home.'

"But in the long voyage over the Pacific, Danny asked me to read to him again the book, *Sir Knight of the Splendid Way*. After many terrible battles and experiences, there met him at the crossroads a fine handsome knight named Sir Plaudio. 'What a gallant life you have led,' cried out Sir Plaudio. 'You must take it easier now. You deserve it. You have earned it.'

"Sir Plaudio's words sounded like the voice in my own heart, but as we turned the pages we discovered that he was really *self* in its final disguise! The Lord laid His finger on this.

"Another day I came upon Matthew 10:23, and I noticed that the Lord did *not* say, 'When they persecute you in one place, go hom and stay home.' He said, 'Go into another.'

"Finally, to cap it all, I was given Amy Carmichael's book *Figures of the True*. In it is a picture of a great snow-peaked mountain. (It brought back quick memories of Pien Ma Pass, where we were caught in a sleet storm, and it was necessary to press on or perish.)

" 'Climb or die,' said Amy Carmichael briefly. And I knew she was right. One could stay home and seek ease, but it is possible to keep the form of piety, but to dry up inside until one is hard and brittle—useless to God or man. . . . When does the life of God pour through you richly? When you accept the challenge of a new thing for Him! 'Climb or die!' It was His final word to me."

CHAPTER SIX

WITH PURPOSE OF HEART

PULLING harder than love of home, children and country was her "first avowed intent to be a pilgrim."

"Kathryn's graduation from college is now a happy memory . . . then came the goodbye." So it was that in July, 1952 Isobel wrote to her praying constituency, "Inch by inch the Plush Curtain is being pushed aside that we may go through and out. The luxury of family life we are forgoing for His sake. . . . Goodbye to our dear little home in Wheaton and to friends!"

Vigilant mother that she was, Isobel made a hurried trip across the States to tuck Danny into the wide-open home of her old friends, Dr. and Mrs. Willard Aldrich. The fact that they already had nine children of their own did not limit the hospitality of the Aldriches![1] Their door stood ajar to Kathy too, who was studying at Multnomah School of the Bible.

With their children settled, John and Isobel faced the inevitable packing, speaking engagements and farewells. But in spite of all the details they had to attend to before leaving America, they procured some language records and even began work on the new Thai lessons. But when the French ship *Liberte* sounded its solemn warning for departure and slipped from its dock in New York harbour, John and Isobel were aboard bound for the Orient via England and the Continent.

All along their way they added more friends. First it was at the London headquarters of the C.I.M. Then at the Abergele Prayer Conference in North Wales. There they met the leaders of the C.I.M. prayer groups from all over England. "A unique conference," wrote Isobel. "It was held in a beautiful estate, Clarendon School for Girls, so secluded from the world and its rush that missionaries and prayer partners get closer together

---

[1] Dr. Aldrich is president of the Multnomah School of the Bible in Portland, Oregon.

than I have ever experienced before." While visiting in England there were also long and thrilling hours with the widow and young daughters of J. O. Fraser, the pioneer of Lisuland, so dear to the Kuhns.

Stopping next in Holland, then early in August in Switzerland, where the Home Director, Mr. Emanuel Baumann, and his wife made them tremendously welcome, Isobel commented, "Switzerland is Lisuland come back . . . only civilized, and in some places even more beautiful." She had been speaking with the help of an interpreter in a meeting there one day. At the end of the service many smilingly greeted her in German, a language Isobel did not understand. But one lady addressed her warmly and in clear English. Isobel never forgot her. "Dear Ma-ma," she said, "I love you from your books."

So they were made keenly aware of Christian kinship wherever they were. Although their destination was half a world away from their most precious possessions—their children—yet in their Father's family, unfolding before them, was fulfilled Christ's promise of a hundredfold compensation. "And every one that hath forsaken houses, or brethren, or sisters, or father, or mother, or wife, or children, or lands, for my name's sake, shall receive an hundredfold" (Matt. 19:29). Who could ask greater recompense?

From Marseilles to Thailand, the Kuhns' journey was entirely by water. While trans-shipping in Singapore, they consulted about their future assignment with the staff officers at the newly established headquarters of the C.I.M. Then sailing on through tropical seas they finally entered the mouth of the Chao Phraya River. There Isobel had her first view of Thai life as the ship wedged its way through crowded cargo craft, and edged past twenty miles of thatched shanties, coconut groves and dense green jungle. Near the port of Bangkok the sharp spires of Buddhist temples rose from the panorama like the spears of an army of giants. Yellow-robed priests were everywhere in the city. But soon the missionaries left Bangkok behind as they boarded a northbound train for Chiengmai, in north Thailand, their destination.

"As John Kuhn took up the responsibilities of superintendent of this tribal area, Isobel made Chiengmai, hub of the tribal work, 'home' to all the workers." So wrote Eileen O'Rourke,[1] herself a tribal worker and a close friend of Isobel's.

"Many a weary missionary reaching Chiengmai tired, dusty, muddy, and footsore from long treks, would know the grip of a hand and the joy of being welcomed, not only into a home but into a heart.

"Days could be very hectic in Chiengmai for the superintendent's wife! Constant comings and goings, ordering stores for the outstations, sending off bundles of mail to isolated missionaries, securing language teachers for new workers who made Chiengmai their base, and numerous other tasks, which used up the minutes of the day. But she always gave the time to sit down, listen, pray, weep and rejoice with the incoming warrior. Sympathy and encouragement were always found in her heart. The sympathy was not the weak 'Pity thyself' type, but the strong sympathy of fellowship in enduring suffering for His name's sake. And encouragement came as she turned her eyes towards her Beloved and revelled in His good purposes which lay just ahead.

"In the hot tropical climate, when others were taking their short time of rest after the noonday meal, Mr. and Mrs. Kuhn would keep their daily tryst with God as they prayed for their fellow-workers on the surrounding mountain-sides. The knowledge of these intimate prayers that surrounded each worker was a strengthening factor in many a missionary's battle."

And surely, spiritual battles rage on those eerie hillsides. The Ancient Foe storms away at God, the Mighty Fortress. The tribes are not easily won to Christ: they have no written language, they worship demons, they deeply involve themselves in the opium traffic—smoking it, growing it, smuggling it. Of course, the missionaries, few and scattered as they are, feel like grasshoppers in their sight except as God reassures them that they are fighting under the shelter of the "Bulwark never failing . . . and He must win the battle."

So the superintendent and his wife assumed the work of prayer as one of their major responsibilities for helping their fellow-workers.

"It is probably her prayer life that stands out most in people's

---

[1] August 30, 1958, Miss O'Rourke became Mrs. J. B. Kuhn.

memories of Isobel, a disciplined prayer life that trained her for immediate access to the King at any time," said Nurse Dorothy Jones. "Up each morning at five-thirty, she kept a careful watch over her bed time to ensure this. Missionaries and tribal Christians were prayed for by name; problems and difficulties brought before the Lord; hard places wept over. We were all accustomed to praying with her over matters that arose and it was not uncommon when talking to find one's words suddenly interrupted by 'Let's pray about it.' Days were set apart for this special ministry. It meant a lot for missionaries in their tribal villages to know there was someone to whom one could write anything and everything, to know such letters were spread before the Lord, and also to receive answers not written just to soothe or comfort if a stimulant seemed necessary."

Isobel dealt with herself as faithfully as she dealt with others, as Mrs. Orville Carlson adds, "I believe the inward life of prayer gave a daily victory. . . . She told me how she had to fight self-pity all her life. Another thing she fought was mental depression. From her bright ways, one would never have thought these things to be difficulties. Her own testimony to me was that the Lord never removed this from her; it had to be a daily commitment to Him."

A visitor in 1952, Dr. A. J. Broomhall,[1] remarked, "What struck me particularly about her was the strength of personality that was apparent in her, as well as a high spiritual standard. Whatever she turned her hand to she seemed to know exactly what she wanted to do and to approach it with definite suggestions about getting down to prayer or taking some practical action on the matter."

Of course "Home Base" as the house came to be called, was primarily for the convenience of C.I.M. personnel—men like Dr. Broomhall, on Mission business; young missionaries based there for language study; others in transit who came and went to their out-of-the-way places of service. Sometimes staff members came from Singapore. Annually a field conference convened there for the available C.I.M. workers in North Thailand.

Occasionally there was a distinguished guest to entertain,

---

[1] Author of *Strong Tower* and *Strong Man's Prey*.

someone making a world survey of mission fields. Once in a
while a lone globe-trotter dropped in, like the young lady from
the United States doing a world tour on her own. She called
herself an agnostic, so Isobel had little in common with her. But,
discovering a common interest in elephants, Isobel led her visitor
off to find some of the big beasts at work. This excursion
provided the missionary-hearted Isobel with her desired opportunity to chat personally with the empty-hearted girl about the
Saviour, all-sufficient.

So Isobel entertained guests various and sundry. Sometimes the
place seemed like a small hotel! This large scale housekeeping was
exactly what Isobel least liked when long years before she had had
a taste of it in China. She greatly preferred the direct teaching
work with the tribal people. Yet now in Thailand she not only
accepted her new position gladly but also carried off her responsibilities graciously. She even had studied away at the Thai
language until she could make herself quite intelligible in
managing the house servants and tradespeople.

It was no small task to supervise her Thai servants in their
round of purchasing, preparing and serving of food, and in their
laundering of clothes that so soon mounted into sodden piles if
not promptly cared for in that tropical heat. And to Isobel,
"servants were not just employees," as Nurse Dorothy Jones
observed. "Each one was a real responsibility to the missionary
who employed them. Reckoning accounts with the Christian
cook led into many more matters than so many pounds of rice at
so much a pound.

"One Sunday morning one of the servants was being admitted
into church membership. She had believed only a short while
and this was a big day for her. Mission-family prayers were
interrupted while Isobel gave her a word of encouragement,
prayed with her and saw her off down the road. Later she was
given a course of Bible study when on regular nights each week
she turned up with Bible and notebook for instruction."

Many women under similar circumstances would have declared they had no opportunity for this direct type of missionary
work. But not Isobel. She prayed for opportunities and seized
them eagerly.

"Alert."

This was the one word that seemed most to characterize Isobel in the mind of Mr. Herbert Griffin, now for many years Home Director for the C.I.M. in North America.

In spite of her duties as hostess in Chiengmai Isobel refused to become bound to the house where traditionally "a woman's work is never done." Instead she made long weary trips to strange settlements. She mentions one day's trek of seventeen miles. Sometimes she introduced young women workers to their first strange tribal living, then fluttered her mother wings over them in their new experiences. Together they encountered discomfort, fatigue and danger. Her singing helped them, as Eileen O'Rourke mentioned, "Out on the trail wending towards a distant village, it was Isobel Kuhn's voice first which would be raised in song that floated back to those who followed single file, making it easy to worship the One we loved together. One of her favourites was:

> "Rivers to the ocean run
>   Nor stay in all their course,
> Fire ascending seeks the sun
>   Both speed them to their source.
> So my soul, derived from God,
>   Pants to see His glorious face.
> Forward tends to His abode
>   To rest in His embrace."
>
> *Anon.*

The last few lines of the song held deep significance.

But panting along in the heat of the tropics, little did any of the party foresee how soon Isobel's panting soul might rest literally in her Lord's embrace!

CHAPTER SEVEN

THE RULING THING

IT was one day out on the trail. In fact, it was Isobel's first trip in North Thailand in search of tribal people. Plagued with hindrances, annoyances and misfortunes, the little group gathered together with her on the steep jungle-tangled mountainside to ask God's special protection for each member of the party.

It happened *not before*, but *after* that prayer of faith.

They were walking single file. A fallen tree branch lay concealed under the leaves on the path. Suddenly someone in front of her unwittingly stepped on the one end, causing the other tō spring up, striking her sharply on the breast.

As almost any other woman might react, Isobel was immediately suspicious of what an injury to that vulnerable spot might bring in its wake. But painful as it was, she completed the trip with the others. And returning to the city she consulted Dr. Richard Buker.[1] He gave it as his opinion that a ligament had been torn by the blow. After this verdict, putting the matter from her mind, Isobel went on with her usual programme.

Seven months passed. Again on a trip to the tribes, she had an accident. She fell on a slippery slope, striking herself painfully again.

"Down I came on a jagged stump," she explained. "It was a jolting blow and fell in the same place as the first. Once down the

---

[1] At that time Dr. Richard Buker, an American Baptist missionary, was serving under the American Presbyterian Board in Chiengmai. There in the McKean Memorial Hospital he headed up one of the world's largest leprosy colonies. From Dr. and Mrs. Buker as well as others of the A.P.M., the C.I.M. received a genuine welcome to North Thailand. They were as glad to have the assistance of the C.I.M. medical personnel as the C.I.M. appreciated access to their facilities. It is to Dr. Buker that the C.I.M. owes both the pattern and training for its successful leprosy programme in Thailand. To use simple leprosy clinics as a spearhead into unevangelized areas, was Dr. Buker's idea.

hill I again sought advice. An X-ray showed nothing. I felt as if the Lord said, 'The time hasn't come yet; get on with your work.' And so I did. I was not haunted by any fear of the disease —I had put it deliberately out of my mind and was joyful in my work. Over a year passed. I had never felt better in my life. But one day, noticing something not normal in the area where twice I had been hit, I felt I should see Dr. Buker." He looked very serious and ordered further investigation immediately. This necessitated a trip to Bangkok.

When "non-malignant" came as the first report, John naturally was jubilant. Friends were all tremendously thankful; those at Home Base were specially reassured as Isobel returned to Chiengmai and to her usual rhythm.

Yet, somehow, she herself was still unconvinced. In spite of this, she pressed on.

"Our annual Field Conference was coming very close," she said, "and I threw my energies into preparing for it. We house-cleaned every room, and all arrangements were clearly mapped out even to the menu for each day."

A busy week passed. Then came Saturday with the dramatic incidents remembered so vividly by Nurse Dorothy Jones. "We were awaiting guests for supper, and in walked Dr. Buker. He had news that all was not well as first supposed and a surgeon from Bangkok who had just flown up for a forty-eight-hour break would be willing to operate on the following day. What does one do with guests when a major operation is suddenly arranged for the hostess on the next day?

"Once again we were privileged to see God's peace in action, for according to Isobel, the hostess welcomed the guests and gave them an enjoyable evening. Next morning at half-past seven we drove to hospital in the jeep and the operation was performed. Then came days of pain and discomfort, days when there was plenty of time to think of the future, of loved ones; and the strength was given. Then the day came for her home-coming and she said she would go into her own prayer sanctuary —a little room away from the house, with thatched roof, walls of bamboo slats and earth floor. The nurse said, 'Nonsense, no patient of mine can go in there.' But the patient knew better. And the doctor realized the value of a room away from the main house with its much coming and going (for conference was to begin that week-end). So into that little sanctuary Isobel went.

"One day the soap dropped on the floor. Soap on a wood or a stone floor is one thing, one just picks it up and continues washing. But soap on an earth floor is another thing, the soap needs washing before going on with its work. 'Oh well,' said the nurse, 'only a few more days and you'll be enjoying the comfort of a New York hospital.' 'I'd rather be here in this little sanctuary,' was the reply. And Isobel meant it. She had spoken before of 'miserable comforts' as she was kept in the centre where living was more civilized. Her heart was out in the hills with her Lisu.

"I don't suppose we shall ever assess fully what her presence meant during conference time. At first no visitors were allowed. But later she could see people a little each day. And those who went to see her found the same Isobel, one ready to advise, to encourage, to exhort. The last night of conference we met around the Lord's Table and she joined us."

Needless to say, at that last observance of the Lord's Supper there was a poignant sense of oneness with the Lord Jesus in His suffering and death for the sins of the whole world. For that sacred hour, the Lord in His perfect planning and time provided His special messenger, Dr. Frank Torrey, John's and Isobel's own pastor from the Calvary Independent Church in Lancaster, Pennsylvania! He was visiting the missionary members of his church scattered around the world; and he reached Chiengmai just when his presence and prayers meant the most.

The next day Isobel started out on the long flight to the States, still very weak in body, but radiant in spirit.

The doctors felt that if she had a chance for recovery it would be by means of new therapies in her homeland.

Isobel, quite aware of the grave nature of her disease, did not shift her vision to herself. That was evident from a message she sent the Mission family in Chiengmai on her last evening in Bangkok. Concluding her letter she wrote:

"I thank the Lord for each one of you and would leave you Philippians 3:13, 14: 'Brethren . . . this one thing I do, forgetting those things which are behind. . . . I press toward . . . Christ Jesus.' Let that be *the ruling thing* in your life as I wish it to be in mine."

CHAPTER EIGHT

CONFIDENT

THE plane taxied into position on the Bangkok airfield. In the little group encircling Isobel Kuhn, throats were tight, eyes moist, feelings deep.

Gazing at each other, husband and wife must have wondered when, if ever, they would be together again. They were doing what they had determined not to do, agreeing to another protracted separation. Between them there was the understanding that John would serve another year until usual furlough was more nearly due, provided Isobel responded to the new therapy. But if she did not, he would fly to her immediately.

In good spirits that morning Isobel wired to Chiengmai Psalm 108:1, "O God, my heart is fixed; I will sing and give praise." The Lord was giving her inner strength as much prayer focused upon her. The Mission had arranged that Nurse Barbara Morgan, who was about due for furlough at that time, should accompany Isobel as far as London.

Final goodbyes were said and blue skies opened to the travellers. Then when the roar of the plane's engines faded into dead silence, friends dispersed. And John Kuhn strode off like a soldier. Back he went to his desk, his lone vigils and long treks in the mountains.

On November 14, 1954, just three weeks after her serious surgery in North Thailand, Isobel flew in to Idlewild airport, New York. As she scanned the faces of the waiting crowd, she recognized three; her own Kathy, Elden Whipple (son of Julia Whipple, Isobel's "spiritual mother"), and Elden's wife Marian. After helping her through landing formalities they assisted the traveller to their car and sped her to Philadelphia.[1] At once she was wrapped in the embraces of friends who had long loved and

[1] Headquarters for the C.I.M. in North America, where Mr. Whipple is Candidates Secretary.

prayed for her. How unspeakably grateful she was for the security the Mission Home afforded her as a member of the Mission. "The bosom of the Mission family is a wonderful place," she said.

Best of all was to have her daughter right with her. "I arrived two days after our Kathryn was accepted by the C.I.M., with prospects of sailing in February. It is unending joy for me to have her companionship. Truly the Lord has been good to me." And Isobel quoted the R. A. Knox version of 2 Timothy 1:12, "I am not put to the blush. He to whom I have given my confidence is no stranger to me."

No; "no stranger." The Lord had schooled her for thirty years and she had discovered that confidence in Him is always rewarding. So now, enrolled in His finishing school, her advanced testings did not floor her.

She wrote to her prayer partners, "John and I are anxious that this news should not cast a gloom over you. There is no gloom in our hearts; there is no gloom in His heart as He watches over me —why should there be in yours? Look up for His direction in praying for me; that is all."

There was certainly no trace of gloom about the letter she soon sent to her friends in tribesland. Whimsical, it came right out of her Irish heart! "When I get to heaven," she smiled, "all they will see of me will be my feet, for my body will be dangling over the parapets looking at you all in North Thailand!" Her interest in them led her to write generous reams about their prayer needs to her praying friends. Probably those friends preferred hearing the details about Isobel's own health, and family, but usually she reserved only a few lines to speak of herself. Yet actually her own needs were acute. Her case was in the hands of an excellent cancer specialist, who was doing all in his power to relieve her; but the required treatments at the University Hospital where she went two or three times a week, were severely upsetting.

In her ups and downs, the Lord had His own satisfying way of comforting Isobel. For instance, when Christmas holidays came, some gracious friend conceived the plan of paying Danny's plane fare, hurrying the eleven-year-old across from coast to coast into his mother's arms. How rich she felt with both her children near! Especially she leaned on Kathy—"hands and feet to Mommie," Isobel exulted.

But the days were galloping along toward Kathy's sailing date. Although Isobel's health was improving, she couldnot expect to live until her "Girlie" returned from a term on the mission field. So one thing was practically certain; this parting would be final. Kathryn believed God wanted her to go without delay. She was prepared to stay, however, if her mother said so.

Conflict began to build up as pros and cons flashed through Isobel's mind. On the one hand she wanted the girl to go. Had she not been dedicated to the Lord from the very hour of her birth? And after all, as another had expressed it, "Is anything too precious to give to Jesus?" But——! Must Kathy leave *now*? If ever a mother needed her daughter was it not *now*?

Isobel faced the climacteric decision.

She was human. She was strongly tempted to delay Kathryn. Years before when Isobel herself was a daughter leaving her mother and home under somewhat similar circumstances, she went straight ahead to do what she believed God wanted her to do. Now when Isobel was the mother in the case, what did she do? She did the same thing! And through repeated experiences of proving God's way perfect, she yielded to Him in good spirit.

"Goodbye, little Daughter," she headed her letter telling the story:

"It took place after everyone had gone to bed one night. The time had come when a final decision must be made—was Kathryn to sail on 24th February or not? There was only One who held the answer, so I asked Him to give it to me, plainly, so I could make no mistake. Immediately He gave me Luke 14:26. Knox's version reads, 'If any man comes to me, without hating his . . . children . . . yes, and his own life too, he can be no disciple of mine.'

"It pierced the mother-side of me, but I had asked Him for a straight word. I quivered a moment, then prayed, 'All right, Lord. But please could you give me another word—just for me myself?' And just as quickly He gave me 1 Peter 2:3, 4a— 'You have surely tasted the goodness of the Lord. Draw near to Him.' It was enough—a dear familiar pillow on which to rest my head.

"As a mother, don't I shrink from sending such a young girl out to the war-threatened Orient in these days? On my calendar one day this month there was this text and comment on Mark 14:5: 'It might have been sold. But thank God, it wasn't.' What if Mary of Bethany had used her alabaster box for herself? And I shuddered to think of the loss it would have been to us all. Mary's sacrifice has sent many a young life to the ends of the earth with the message of salvation. And I have myself seen what her story has meant to those on the far hilltops of Lisuland. So I echoed devoutly, 'Thank God, it wasn't.' Only a girl, only one young life, but none of us can measure what He can do with it.

"Kathryn and I are both emotional by nature; our hearts are easily rent and we suffer deeply. Our friends have been praying for us and I want to tell you how wonderfully God has answered. First of all we faced the fact together that the indulgence of grief profits nothing and can do much harm to the nervous system. It is always hardest for the one left behind, for memory can claw at the heart. Because of this we planned to say the real goodbye in our bedroom in Philadelphia. Then I went to the ship, but did not stay to see it sail. I went on board and saw her cabin, met her cabinmates and then left with a friend. The next day my friend put me on a train and I came on here to Wheaton and Danny.

"I have since had a letter from Kathryn, mailed from Halifax, and she said, 'Mummy, I didn't shed a tear when the ship pulled out.' For Kathryn, this is a miracle, and we thank those who prayed. Such self-discipline does not make the heart hard or shallow. I have had eighteen years of it, and I know. But it saves nervous strength for situations where tension is inescapable. Even so, without the Lord's help, such discipline is not possible."

Perhaps it helped both mother and daughter to know that Kathy would be welcomed in Singapore by her father. John Kuhn had just arrived there, where he served temporarily on the Headquarters Staff as an Assistant Overseas Director. Meanwhile, Danny, after the Christmas holidays, had the good care of the Ernest Carlburgs, house parents in the C.I.M. children's hostel in Wheaton.

After Kathy's sailing Isobel went to tuck Dan under her

motherly wing, and settle into her Wheaton home nest at 123 Scott Street. By that time she was feeling the benefit of the Philadelphia therapy and strong enough to do some light house-keeping.

In a letter giving a picture of her fledgling she gives one of herself too.

"Each morning as Dan disappears down the three flights of steps, he calls back, 'Mom! May I bring one of the fellows home from school today?' (If Mom's larder is flourishing there will be a treat for them!) That day it was Phil Cox he had in tow, next day it was David Rockness." Both were sons of C.I.M. missionaries. Isobel not only ransacked her refrigerator for them, but held them enthralled with true stories of their parents' hair-breadth experiences in China.

But that was Isobel; always out-going to young people! For years she had more than entertained Dan by reading to him. As he curled up beside her they shared many hours of close comradeship.

Isobel organized her time so she could also work at her writing. For a pastime in Philadelphia she had begun the chapters included as Part Two in this volume. Now she put the Vistas aside for more serious work on *Ascent to the Tribes*,[1] considered one of her best books. She finished it that year of 1955.

During the summer Isobel spent some time in New York State and Pennsylvania. Beside checking again with her specialist in Philadelphia, she had some speaking engagements at conferences. For years she and Miss Bessie Traber, founder of the Bible Club Movement, had strengthened one another's hands in the Lord, like David and Jonathan. Miss Traber invited her to give the missionary addresses at the B.C.M. Senior Camp and also the Leaders' Camp. But the dates so nearly coincided with those of her next engagement that Isobel needed to make quick connections. To help her, George Sutherland, who had been "Uncle George" to Kathy for years, offered to chauffeur Isobel from Camp Sankanac to Keswick Grove, New Jersey.

At the Camp one day, Isobel got a long distance call from Mr. Sutherland. After some of his characteristic banter, he completely

[1] Published 1956 by Moody Press in U.S.A. and by the C.I.M. in Great Britain.

overwhelmed her with great news: her husband had cabled. At that moment John was hopping across oceans and continents to reach her. Due to arrive soon!

When John came in at the airport George Sutherland was there to meet him. He telephoned Isobel at once. Adding Mrs. Sutherland to the party, they drove like racers to the Camp. At the end of the road John saw his wife waiting for him on the porch. With quick steps they were united; thankful pounding hearts were close, exuberant!

In all the joy of that day, however, no one could quite forget a haunting fact—John and Isobel Kuhn were facing one more separation.

When would that last parting come?

As they stood side by side on the Keswick platform their victorious spirit gave emphasis to every word they said. In that sacred session there was hardly a dry eye in the room. God was glorified. Who could deny that a God "able to save after this sort" is a great God of wonders, worthy of the utmost confidence? The witness of their lives and lips was wholly convincing.

After that conference John and Isobel stopped to share their experiences with their fellow-missionaries at the C.I.M. in Philadelphia. Isobel, pretty in a flowery hat, was pink-cheeked and gay with excitement. She looked remarkably well and strong. In November she wrote, "We give thanks for the Lord's goodness in supplying strength to keep our autumn speaking schedules. Mine was very light perforce, but at Washington, Philadelphia, and Lancaster areas it was possible to meet with praying friends and mutually encourage one another."

On one of those Sundays in autumn, Isobel spoke in a service where the writer and her husband were present. We were impressed both with the simplicity of her message and its influence as we felt the grip of the Holy Spirit on our hearts that morning.

Meeting her again in Wheaton, Isobel, in a private conversation, mentioned that her trouble was progressing and that the doctor advised further surgery. "I'm not going to have it," she declared. Of course, like anyone else she dreaded the ordeal. But for a different reason she was ready to forego the relief it might give. "It wouldn't be a cure, just arrest the trouble temporarily, and prolong my life. As it is, I'm an expense to the Mission, and detaining John from going back to the field work."

It was a reaction typical of Isobel's attitude; conscientious about the Mission's treasury, and concerned that the Gospel have every priority.

"But Isobel," I protested strongly, "your life is too valuable to the Mission not to extend it if possible! Don't you realize that what you say now has ten times the significance it had when you were able-bodied? Besides, what about your writing? Why not write your own life story?" (At that time I had no idea that I would ever be entrusted with her biography.) There were only a few minutes for our intense conversation. I felt convinced that Isobel inwardly yearned for an incentive to go on living. Essentially she *needed to be needed*. Later, when she sought and found the Lord's guidance, she dropped me a note.

"I am to be operated on after all by Dr. Adolph's colleague on 31st December at 8 a.m., and it is partly the result of your last talk with me. As you suggested another book, the Lord gave me the theme for one! But I had no time to write before Christmas. I had to prepare for company. The Harrisons and Jacksons[1] were with us and we had a wonderful time. But the disease is growing rapidly, and I knew if I were to go on writing *after* Christmas something must be done to retard it. So I consented to the surgery. I know you will pray and ask others to. And then pray for leisure and strength to write? If it is His will."

Comparative well-being followed.

Quite conscious, however, that her life could not continue very much longer, she wrote her brother Murray a letter unique in expression of confidence in the Lord. This he kindly offered for use in this story.

"February 18, 1956

"My dear Murray,

"Thank you so much for writing to me the kind of letter you thought I would prefer. I did, and appreciate it very much.

"I think the difference between our faiths is that mine has led

[1] John Kuhn's sister and brother-in-law and their married daughter and her husband.

me to *know God*. You say that you have felt rebellious at what has happened to me, but I don't feel the least so! I have proved God so often that I know He only chooses the best for me. I do not say He chose this disease, but He *allowed* it. When He allows an evil, it is for the purpose of bringing *greater* blessing than if it had not happened. He makes Satan overstep himself and then takes spoils from him.

"I was startled at first, to hear that I was not going to live. But then—I never did want to live till I grew feeble and useless. How grateful I am that that is not to be! To be allowed to die in harness was always a dear hope of mine, and God is granting it. Although I have discomfort I am not in actual pain yet, and I am able to write for the Mission. Just because I am sick people value what I write twice as much as they did before, so I feel that I am still earning my way, so to speak. The Mission would support me in any case, but it is a very happy thing to me to be able to do something of value.

"I thoroughly enjoy each day. I am not allowed out, but I have big sunny windows with a pleasant view, and my room is full of flowers. Everybody is so kind to me. People I don't know, but who have heard me speak, send me things. I lack nothing I could wish for. The Lord is so good to me.

"You say I have a life well-lived. I am glad that I gave my life to Christ when I was young, but that is not my satisfaction. I am trusting only in Christ's merits for salvation; my own life has been too full of faults and failures to be worth anything.

"But because I have had daily fellowship with God (through Christ), I expect to have it on the Other Side. And I know God so well that I am sure He will have delightful work for me to do Up There. The Bible does not teach that, but experience with God makes me sure it will be so. And then I have so many dear ones in heaven. Besides Father and Mother, there are many Lisu whom I love dearly, and even one from Thailand. So the other side of the dark valley is very bright. There will be that period of pain first, and I appreciate your prayers that it be short. I am no heroine, and don't look forward to it. But once there, the Lord will surely have help for me. He has never failed me nor forsaken me. So you see I have every reason to be happy. Danny would be my biggest reason for wanting to stay, of course. But having a mother in heaven may help him spiritually—how do I know? I know I can trust the dear Lord who has guided me unfailingly up to now.

"I don't know how people face life with its trials without Him. I know many just try *not to think*. That is so sad to me. When they could have this wonderful moment by moment fellowship and comradeship. I am so grateful He led me to Himself when I was young so that I could have this long earthly walk with Him. I recommend Him as a peerless Master.

"The doctor has been giving me some new medicine that has slowed things up a little, and given me a bit of temporary strength. Otherwise I do not write personal letters but save my strength for the writing for the Mission.

"I do appreciate your love and this handshake across the continent, and I send mine in return. John and Danny join me with much love.

"Your little sister,
"Isobel."

In this mood, Isobel's letter echoed one written by St. Paul long ago when he quietly said, "We are confident, I say, and willing rather to be absent from the body and to be present with the Lord. Wherefore we labour, that, whether present or absent, we may be accepted of Him."

Isobel lived just a year and a month after writing the letter to her brother. She hardly expected to live that long.

CHAPTER NINE

IN CHRIST'S COMPANY

"YE will not get leave to steal quickly to Heaven, in Christ's company, without a conflict and a cross" (*Samuel Rutherford*). Isobel borrowed joy from companionship with Christ and from the sure hope He set before her. For years He had been known to her as the Alpha, the author of her faith. Now she trusted Him as the Omega, its finisher. She held fast her confidence in His great objective—He would one day present her faultless before the presence of God's glory with exceeding joy. She dared believe this, imperfect as she was; for she had the assurance of Scripture in Jude 24!

Meanwhile her loss of health brought about much gain for Christ.

Her last months were like an autumn with its highest colours and fullest fruit. Almost daily she worked away at her writing with much steady purpose and self-discipline. And she enjoyed it. "To go back over God's dealings with me," she commented, "and His multitudinous lovingkindnesses is in itself a thrill and a blessing. How good is the God we adore!" With satisfaction she went on to say, "We have a little four-roomed apartment, and a home to ourselves is a luxury which I have learned to appreciate. Always on the field we had fellow-workers living with us, and hardly ever knew the privacy of a meal just to ourselves."

Above the Kuhns' apartment, Ella Graham made her home on the third floor. She and Isobel had long been friends having roomed together in Language School in China. Now as Isobel's strength ebbed, Ella's sympathy flowed. Selflessly she prepared meals, kept the house, shopped and nursed. Surely through Mrs. Graham, His ministering angel, the Lord bore the invalid's grief and carried her sorrows right to the end! Without this willing help Isobel never could have written three books and part of a fourth during that year of 1956.

Quite a bit of her life story she scattered in three of these books. "I have always been inclined to criticize people who wrote themselves up," she admitted. "Or allowed biographies to be printed while they were alive. The Lord could never have persuaded me to write mine if He had not done just what He did do—tied me up to this and only this, with the promise that I'd be away before it came out in print!"

There were still some things unsaid, however. So the writer as her biographer was commissioned to gather them together with other available materials, to snip and sew them into one whole story. In this project, both John and Isobel were very co-operative.

In November, 1956 we went to Wheaton with Mr. and Mrs. Herbert Griffin especially to see the invalid. It was then that we observed for ourselves what Mr. Griffin had previously noted— Isobel's ability to suffer and to keep bright about it. She confessed that at first her imagination gave her a bad time. "If I coughed I immediately had lung cancer (although X-rays showed the chest clear). If I had a toothache then I was getting cancer of the mouth. But when I asserted my right to a sound mind (2 Timothy 1:7) these fears left me: 'For God hath not given us the spirit of fear, but of power and of love and of a sound mind.'"

It was not an easy victory nor a battle fought once for all to a finish. Over and over she had to swing at her subtle enemy with the sword of the Lord.

"For me to let myself imagine how or when the end would come was not only unprofitable, it was definitely harmful, so I had to bring my thoughts into captivity that they might not dishonour Christ. The best way to do this, I found, was to engage in some interesting work. It makes for health to have a goal and keep on striving for it. Of course I realize that the Lord has been especially good to me in giving me work which is so congenial."

Usually Isobel reserved the morning hours for writing and did not welcome any interruptions before noon, for she had discovered that afternoon and evening work might result in a restless night. She was expecting us that November morning, however, and gave herself to us. Shortly before our visit, walking had become too painful for her, so she was in bed.

Fresh and attractive in a pretty dressing-gown, she looked so entirely herself that it was almost impossible at first sight to regard her as a mortally sick woman. However, her easy excitability and fatigue was the characteristic of a very ill person.

Her keen mind, however, raced along. Faster than my pencil could follow! When John tried to save her by answering my questions, she would not have it. She took the words out of his mouth! Out rolled the stories. Some were serious, some hilarious; all were fascinating.

But she was suffering and interrupted herself to take a pain pill. Yet she wanted to go on as long as possible.

Neatly placed in a chest drawer of Isobel's room were her diaries, notebooks, photographs and an almost complete file of her circular letters. They dated from her early years as a missionary. How glad she was that once, when war scattered things and people, she mailed these treasures of hers out of China! Without access to them in Wheaton, she never could have put forth such volumes of virile writing.

In the opinion of many her last and most mature work was her best. *Ascent to the Tribes* and *By Searching* are probably unequalled by her earlier writings: and she was able to picture the missionary enterprise in unforgettable words.

And the real marvel is that the pains piercing Isobel's body were not transmitted from her pen to the pages of her books! Though with utmost frankness she shared her trials of past years, she quietly ignored her sick-room miseries. It was an entirely unconscious testimony, impressive and significant. She was like the bird in a lilting verse she once quoted years earlier:

> "Let us learn, like a bird, for a moment to take
>   Sweet rest on a branch that is ready to break,
>   She feels the branch breaking yet calmly she sings,
>   Why fear? Why tremble? She has wings! She has wings!"
>
> *Anon.*

On wings of the Spirit she balanced on her breaking branch, John sharing with her hours of prayer. But she did not stop at praying for her beloved Lisu, she kept on corresponding with them. Also she contributed articles to *Spiritual Food*, a mimeographed periodical especially designed to encourage the tribal

Christian refugees who had slipped into Burma over China's back wall of mountains. Some of the Lisu responses—Lucius' letter, for instance—thrilled her: "All the evangelists are safe and the R.S.B.S. began with nearly eighty students." And he mentioned 30 villages in his circuit, 270 Christian families, 700 baptisms! And this was a *one hundred per cent indigenous harvest.* Of course such zeal all grew from seed planted and tilled originally by J. O. Fraser, the Allyn Cookes, John and Isobel Kuhn and others of the pioneer missionary group. In cultivating the southwest China field, their work was not in vain in the Lord. This Isobel knew.[1]

No wonder Isobel could declare that though she had less and less strength and more and more pain, "These cancer years have been among my happiest"!

Topping all else came the glad news of Kathryn's engagement to a missionary after their own heart, Donald Rulison. "I just sing with joy for Don and Kathy," the mother exulted. "We love Don and our hearts rest in the thought of him taking care of our Kathy." At once the parents sent off the wedding dress.

Isobel's 55th birthday, a cheery one, was followed by a Christmas, merry with family fellowship and worship. Isobel was up and in her wheel chair.

Then in a *Prayer Trust* letter for January 1, 1957, Isobel wrote, "My verse for the New Year is Isaiah 46:9, 10, 'I am God, and there is none like me. Declaring the end from the beginning. . . . My counsel shall stand, and I will do all my pleasure.' It is wonderful to have the guidance of one's life determined by One who knows the future as well as the past. *There is rest in turning over the helm to Him.*

---

[1] But what she did not then know was that Lisu Job Fish (who had once saved her life) would make his way to North Thailand in 1957. She did not know that he would be joined by another evangelist and that these two tribesmen would collaborate with the Allyn Cookes and the Allan Cranes in translating the Old Testament into the Lisu script. She did not know that in 1958 the Lord would answer another of the prayers of years by bringing four brave Lisu over the mountains on a visit from Burma, to help to evangelize the demon-worshipping Lisu of North Thailand.

"So Ho! for the Pilot's orders
Whatever course He takes—
For *He sees beyond the skyline*
And He never makes mistakes."

and she signed the letter, "Yours in the certainties of Calvary."

Finally one day in February Isobel laid down her pen. She closed the large loose-leaf binder she had been using while finishing the Intimate Vistas. Her handwriting had become increasingly cramped and illegible towards the end of the manuscript and she condensed her conclusion as if hurrying to a close.

And the pen dropped from her hand.

Had not she herself, like a pen in God's hand, written the name of Jesus on many a heart?

Her life motto, *God first* had become a copy for others to trace after her. Who knows how many missionaries, national and foreign, already have been moved to action by Isobel Kuhn's pointed pen?

But when the pen had to be put aside, her days were filled in with reading, receiving callers and necessarily with more resting.

For a while John and Isobel seemed to be spending their days in an air castle in sunny North Thailand, where the Rulison nuptials were to take place at Chiengmai. Isobel was living for the news of that occasion. And she did not have to wait long. Even the wedding pictures were promptly whisked over the seas by air. And when she slipped them into a folder she had prepared, they fitted exactly!

About that time John wrote to some intimate friends. "We might not have Isobel with us much longer now. . . . It is a satisfaction to be by her side. The grace of the Lord is richly manifested through her."

Then one day Mr. and Mrs. Morris Rockness called, bound for their responsible post at C.I.M. headquarters in Singapore. They were deeply moved as Isobel expressed to them her confidence and longing. It came out in one contented sentence: "Lord, now lettest thou thy servant depart in peace, according to thy word, for mine eyes have seen thy salvation" (Luke 2:29, 30).

Soon after that, God granted Isobel Kuhn's desire. Vision dawned to full realization on March 20, 1957.

In that hallowed hour, her husband was alone with her. His tenderness and quiet strength had supported her right up to the open gates. Hers was not the tragedy of a premature death but the triumph of a fulfilled ministry. "If I was ever near Heaven," he said, "and if I ever was conscious that death has lost its sting, it was then."

ONE VISION ONLY

The story of a girl
who deliberately threw away her life —
and found it.

Isobel Kuhn, as a young graduate, felt called to China
as a missionary. Abandoning the bright career predicted for
her, she started training despite her parents' initial opposition
her ministry with her husband would be to the Lisu tribes,
whom her writings were to bring to international attention,
and to whom she would devote most of her life.

'How could anyone then foresee how remarkably she would
demonstrate one of Christ's greatest paradoxes?' comments
Carolyn Canfield. ' Whosoever will save his life shall lose
it; and whosoever will lose his life for my sake,
shall find it.'

Published jointly with the Overseas Missionary Fellowship.

United Kingdom	£1.25
Rep. of Ireland	£1.37½
Australia (recommended)	$ 3.95
New Zealand	$ 3.95
Canada	$ 3.78

ISBN 0 340 24607 3